Texas Rodeo and Radios Series

Down at the "No Gotty"

Donna Snow King

Texas Rodeo and Radios Series: Down at the "No Gotty"
Donna Snow King
Published December 2025
Little Creek Books
Imprint of Jan-Carol Publishing, Inc.

ISBN: 978-1-970471-13-7
Library of Congress Control Number: On file

You may contact the publisher:
Jan-Carol Publishing, Inc.
PO Box 701
Johnson City, TN 37605
publisher@jancarolpublishing.com
www.jancarolpublishing.com

This book is dedicated to:

Almighty God, who created me; Jesus Christ, who saved me; and

The Holy Spirit, who comforts me.

To my husband, Rex, W5EAK, and my friend Sam, NM5N,

for all your technical help and encouragement in bringing this story to life.

And to Brandy, who is currently working on getting her "ticket."

Thank you for all the hours of reading and re-reading the manuscript.

You are a blessing!

Foreword

After meeting Rex and discovering amateur radio, I soon fell in love with an exciting world I never knew existed. Immediately, I wanted to share it with everyone I met. So, what better way to introduce this amazing hobby than through a story—a story that has more truth than fiction in it.

Rex, W5EAK, was the beginning of this adventure. An adventure I suspect will last for many, many years. He reminded me that you are never too old to learn or too young to teach.

Travel down the road through the twists and turns in this mystery with me, meet some very interesting people, and maybe even laugh a little.

Chapter 1

Donna

Walking up to her truck after filming *Texas Flip N Move* all day in the hot Texas sun, Donna put her work gloves in the toolbox and climbed into her pickup, setting the air conditioning to blow cold and on high. Leaving the production lot, all she could think about was going home, taking a shower, and hitting the hay.

About halfway to the office, she sat straight up, grabbing the steering wheel with both hands, and hollered out loud, "Oh snap, it's Friday night," which meant a watch party down at The BBQ Restaurant in the historic Fort Worth Stockyards. Even as tired as she was, there was no way she was going to miss a watch party. They were always so much fun, and besides that, her sister Toni would kill her—graveyard dead.

Donna and her sister would be watching the newest episode of the show they were on for the first time, along with family, old friends, hopefully some new friends, and anyone else who might stop by. So many times, people would ask them how long it took to memorize their lines for the show. And each time, their answer was the same: "No script, no lines. With us, what you see is what you get." Then the next question would be when they got to view the episode. Again, in unison, their response was always the same: "The same time you do."

The conversation played in Donna's head over and over: "Donna, don't be late. You need to be there early to help set things up." Since she discovered the trip was going to be more than 10 minutes, she reached over and turned on the radio, joining in with the song that was playing, when right in the middle of the song, there was breaking news.

The newsman was giving an update on yet another fentanyl drug incident. Three local teenagers had been found in the alley behind a movie theater. Two of the teenagers had been taken to the local hospital, hanging on by a thread to life, while the third young man was pronounced dead at the scene. The newsman went on to say that local authorities were checking out several leads and would bring the audience any updates as they came in. And just like that, the music began again.

Remembering Toni's instructions, Donna pulled into the parking lot, parking in her usual spot. Seeing her friends from the "P Posse" cars brought her a sigh of relief. Running out of steam was not fun, and she was just about there.

Looking over at the clock in her truck, she soon realized it was going to be close. Talking out loud as if someone were sitting in the truck with her, she said, "Here's me teaching the rodeo team members that arriving 15 minutes ahead of schedule is right on time. However, tonight, I am not setting a good example."

Parked next to her was her friend Rex's SUV with that huge antenna that looked as if it reached all the way up to Heaven. Getting her things out of the truck to head inside, Donna concluded this tall antenna must be for a CB radio system. Smiling to herself, she remembered back in the day having a CB radio and all the fun she had meeting so many people from all across the United States as they traveled through the North Texas area. She decided the best thing to do was just ask Rex about his antenna, thinking it could be fun getting back into that world.

Opening the door and panning the room, there stood Toni with her hands on her hips. As Donna walked up to the main table where everyone was gathered, Miss Bev spoke up and said, "Great timing, Donna. Everything is ready for the watch party."

Looking her straight in the eye, Toni responded, "You better count your blessings that the 'P Posse' handled it all."

The evening's festivities went off without a hitch; it was so much fun. The episode airing was the one where a young couple won a house over in the White Settlement area, where Toni and Donna, along with fellow house mover Randy, brought their lawn chairs and popcorn to watch the fiasco that would unfold in front of their eyes. Randy, Toni, and Donna recognized this episode was about the house that they called "Leaning to the North." And the winning couple of this house had decided to straighten it up before moving it. It seemed they made good on their promise to show up with their lawn chairs and popcorn to watch what they knew would be a train wreck in slow motion.

With everyone's eyes glued to the TV, Randy, Toni, and Donna looked at each other and kinda giggled under their breath remembering what had been happening during filming that day. However, as fast as they started laughing, all three of them stopped and started sucking air when the next scene came on, and it was the scene they had completely expected to be left on the editing room floor. Just as quickly as they stopped laughing, everyone else in the room started laughing hysterically. As far as these three were concerned, crisis averted! With the evening's festivities being over, it was time to clean up and pack up.

"Penny for your thoughts?" Rex asked as he walked up to the table. "May I sit down?"

Looking up at his big 6'5" frame, Donna smiled and said, "Sure thing, my friend. Sit down and take a load off. A penny for my thoughts, you asked? I was reminiscing about all the fun times here at the watch parties–like when we celebrated birthdays by eating cake, celebrated anniversaries by eating cake, and made new friends while creating precious memories. I had always heard to 'feed them, and they would come,' and they did. These special times, money can't buy... Well, except for maybe the cake. Just think, you got all of that for a penny."

Since Donna had Rex's undivided attention, it seemed like a good time to ask him about his humongous antenna. Ronan, his service dog, walked over to her as if wanting to be petted. Since he was a service dog,

Donna knew better, and then there was the patch on his working vest that said, "*Working dog, do not pet.*"

Seeing her hesitation, Rex gave Ronan the command to go "off duty," and she set about petting him. Looking over at Rex, she asked, "Have you ever wondered what dogs are thinking? Take right now as an example. What do you think Ronan is thinking?"

Laughing out loud, Rex remarked, "If he could talk, he would probably say, 'You've got 30 minutes to stop that.'" As they both started laughing, Donna tried to remember a time when she hadn't seen Rex smiling or laughing. It appeared that Rex was not a typical man; in fact, he was very different. He never met a stranger and was so kind to everyone.

"Rex," Donna said, "you are so different from any man I have ever met. I wonder why?"

With the biggest grin on his face, he responded, "Well, I am the world's biggest leprechaun, now, aren't I?"

With a surprised look on her face, she said, "You're Irish?"

"Why, yes I am, on both sides of my family."

Looking over at Rex, Donna continued, "Does that make you full of blarney?"

"So I've been told," he whispered. "So I've been told."

As they both stood up to help carry all the evening's decorations out to Miss Patricia Ann's car, Donna said somewhat anxiously, "Rex, I've been meaning to ask you about that big ole antenna on the front of your SUV. Is that for a CB radio?"

Rex's sweet smile quickly turned to a little bit of a frown as he responded, "No, ma'am, it is not!"

Donna wasn't quite sure what to say as she tried to figure out if he was offended by her question. Not one for too much silence, she continued, "Okay then, other than something to hang wet clothes on to dry when your dryer breaks down, what do you use it for?"

As if coming out of a trance, Rex said, "Why don't you drop over by my house this weekend, and I will explain everything?"

At this point, Donna's curiosity level was right up there with the one that killed the proverbial cat. After a few moments of running her schedule through her mind, she replied, "Sounds good to me, although it will have to be after church on Sunday. I'm all tied up at the high school rodeo on Saturday."

With his smile replacing the frown he had only moments ago, Rex eagerly stated, "Then Sunday it is, after church for both of us."

Chapter 2

Donna

All the usual faces were meeting and greeting one another, patiently waiting for the Sunday morning service to begin. Looking around the auditorium, Donna watched family and friends talking, laughing, and giving each other hugs while Pastor Leo welcomed everyone at the door. Smiling, she suddenly realized that these people were like a second family to her, along with her rodeo family. A family was what she saw before her, even though most of them were not related by blood.

Sheriff Russell and his wife had already taken their usual seats with their son, Houston, sitting over in the "Rodeo Team Row" with his teammates. The Sheriff was one of the most kindhearted people on this earth while still being hard as nails to whomever broke the law. The bottom line was, when the dust settled, he was always fair. The county chose well when they voted Sheriff Russell to head their department.

Walking over to say hello before taking her seat, Donna asked the Sheriff if there had been any updates on the suspected drugs being trafficked through the county. His response was that they were no closer than they were a month ago, and it didn't help that Deputy Weldon was out of town on vacation.

"Vacation?" she asked. "I thought he just got back from a fishing trip."

"As a matter of fact, he did, but then he received an all-expense paid trip to Las Vegas. Evidently, he had signed up in a free drawing and forgot all about it," the Sheriff responded. "And if that wasn't enough, the County Judge and Commissioners Court are on my back night and day. But in their defense, I guess they're probably getting more heat from their constituents."

Looking the Sheriff straight in the eyes, Donna told him that she had faith in him and the Sheriff's department to catch the drug smugglers and get those drugs off the streets.

Glancing over at the rodeo kids' section, a feeling of pride overtook Donna, as her mind played back over the past rodeo seasons watching all the team members as they matured and grew into young adults. She was so proud of Amelia, Greg, Bubba, Alyssa, Houston, Gabe, Ariel, Brady, Maddie, and one of the newest team members, Madison, who was constantly trying to remain a wallflower. Half the time, you never knew she was there, and you could barely hear her speak. Like the rest of the Rodeo Team Sponsors, Donna treated each rodeo kid as if they were her own.

Calling this church her home for many years had brought Donna peace through the ups and downs life had thrown at her. It was in this church she had met many of her friends. One of her very good friends, Anne, who worked at the local bank, and her husband were sitting near the front. And then there was the "Prayer Chain," as they were affectionally known by all members of the church, as well as the community. Rumors went around that they may have been there since the church was founded many years ago. It was clear there was more to these women than what met the eye.

And just like clockwork, as the clock chimed 10 a.m., Pastor Leo took his place at the podium to begin the Sunday service.

Pastor Leo always kept the congregation's attention through his sermons along with some wit sprinkled throughout, but try as she may on this Sunday, Donna's mind couldn't stop from pondering her upcoming afternoon meeting with Rex. So many questions were going through her mind, almost to the point of writing them down so as not to forget one.

Before dismissing the congregation, Pastor Leo reminded everyone about the upcoming church social. The first ones to applaud, as was customary, were of course the Prayer Chain, as they were always in charge of the socials and eagerly looked forward to putting together the menu for the upcoming potluck. It was their opinion that they should be the ones to pick out what dish each family was supposed to bring, basing their decisions on who made what dish the best.

Each lady of the Prayer Chain was most unique in her own right. They were all from different backgrounds, various walks of life, possessing skills and knowledge on just about any subject you would like to discuss. Many times, they showed up right when you needed a little extra help or encouragement. It was almost like they had the answer before a question was asked.

After saying the closing prayer, Pastor Leo quickly made his way to his usual position at the door to wish each family a good day. With all the goodbyes and well wishes done, Donna climbed into her pickup truck with great anticipation of the rest of the day.

* * *

Pulling out of the church parking lot, she called Rex to see if he was home. He answered the phone in his usual cheerful voice: "Well, howdy."

"Hey there, my friend," she responded. "Just checking to see if you are home from church."

"Yes, ma'am, come on over," he replied.

"Well, Rex," she went on to say, "I would, except I have no idea where you live."

"Oh yeah, guess I better text you my address," he said, then added, "You can't miss my house. It's the only one with a flagpole."

"Okie dokie, sir. I have entered it into my navigation system and will see you soon."

Driving through town on Sunday mornings, you could always find Willy on the bench that sat in the shade of the big oak trees around the courthouse. An old, wadded up coat served as his pillow, with a flask at his feet. Some people called him a bum, some called him a hobo, and others called him a transient. Donna called him a lost soul. Willy could be seen walking the streets daily, with his sleeping spots dependent on the weather. Some of the cafés on Main Street that were run by local families always seemed to have extra food left over at the end of the day. The good people of the community were more than glad to give it to him. No one really knew anything about him. For the most part, he never caused a ruckus or trouble. The one thing that stood out to anyone who met him was his piercing blue eyes.

As Donna continued her drive, she soon realized that Rex lived quite a distance from her home—in fact, in a different county, making this drive 47 minutes from her own house, which meant that he drove over an hour to and from each watch party hosted at the barbeque place. She thought this made him a truly dedicated fan of the show. Pondering over what all she knew about Rex, Donna could only come up with three things. One, he was a widower, and from the ball cap he wore, he had served in Vietnam. Lastly, he had a really big service dog, Ronan. Funny thing—he had attended every watch party since Season 1, and this was all she really knew about him.

Entering the subdivision where the navigation system took her, Donna's head bobbed from left to right as if she were at a tennis match. While the homes were big and beautiful, she couldn't help but notice the yards were very small. As a matter of fact, she figured it wouldn't take a hot minute to mow any of them.

Following Rex's instructions, she quickly saw the flags. She pulled up in front of his house and observed the two flags flying so majestically in the summer breeze: the American Flag and the Navy Flag. Walking up the sidewalk to the front door, she rang the doorbell and waited. Within a few moments, there stood Rex and Ronan welcoming her into their home. And once again, Rex was smiling and looked very jovial.

Following them both down the long hallway towards the back of the house, it became evident how lovely and well decorated Rex's place was.

Donna quickly realized this had to be from a woman's touch; Rex was too manly to decorate like this. The walls were covered with military awards, plaques, military recognition certificates, family pictures, and hand oil paintings. She concluded that this home looked like something out of one of those fancy magazines, to the point that she was almost afraid to sit down anywhere.

Walking ahead of her and into the den, Rex pointed to the couch, inviting Donna to sit as he sat in his recliner. She spoke up, "Rex, your home is beautiful."

Smiling as he looked around, he responded, "Thank you, I think it is as well. However, now that I am a widower, well…To be honest, it has become a lot for me to take care of." He went on, "Out of three bedrooms, a den, a kitchen, a formal dining area, an office, and a formal living room, I basically use only a small part of this house. I spend most of my time in my radio shack."

"Radio shack? What's a radio shack?" Donna asked.

Getting up out of his recliner, Rex looked at her and gave her instructions to follow him. "It's actually easier to show you than try and explain it," he said. Heading back down the long hallway towards the front door, he continued, "This will answer your CB radio question from the watch party Friday night."

Reaching into the room and turning on the lights, Rex led her through a set of very ornate, beveled glass French doors. In a faux Irish accent, he welcomed her to his radio shack. Donna could feel the shift of the atmosphere as she entered the room. It was almost like a portal to another time period. Surveying the space, to her left was a large desk that was literally covered with radios left to right, and in some places stacked two high, with what appeared to be a fancy microphone. To the far left of the desk was a desktop computer with a light.

While Donna was not entirely sure what all this equipment was, there was one thing for sure: it sure as heck wasn't a CB radio set-up. Continuing around the room, her eyes came upon two more flags on stands. And again, one was an American Flag, and the other was a Navy Flag. Close to the flags was a sword, and its sheath hung on the wall. Near the sword were two flags folded inside cases with what appeared to be special framed certificates on both sides, as well as various kinds of framed historic military maps.

As Rex sat down in his office chair, he asked, "Well, what do you think?"

Donna finally came back down to earth and jokingly replied, "I feel like a calf staring at a new gate! Wow, Rex! I am blown away."

Smiling with pride, he invited her to sit down in the chair that was across from his. Finding her voice once again, she asked, "What is all of this, sir? I have never seen anything like this before in my life."

"Well, what we have here, Donna, is a 27-inch iMac computer, a YAESU FTM400 VHF/UHF radio, a YAESU FTDX101D HF radio, also referred to as a short-wave radio, connected to a 600-watt amplifier, a tuner which tunes the antenna, a Heil parametric receive audio system and a HS-5 power speaker, a Heil PR781 microphone, with an assortment of antenna switches and lightning arresters. All of this is connected to an 80-10-meter flagpole antenna and a VHF/UHF antenna hidden in the attic."

After listening to him rattle all of those foreign names off, Donna sat there blinking at him before responding, "You lost me after iMac computer, sir. I have no idea what else you just said, but it sure does sound important."

Rex gave her his little-boy sheepish grin and whispered, "It's not much, but it's mine." With half a laugh, he continued, "Want to hear a little funny story about my antenna, Donna?"

Knowing it had to be good, she nodded her head yes.

"Living in an HOA, I wasn't allowed to have what I consider to be a proper antenna. So, I purchased a stealth antenna, which was my flagpole, and no one ever knew. Also, our HOA rules required anyone walking their dog to be on a leash. There was a certain neighbor who always chose to walk his large yellow dog, and as usual, not on a leash. And for whatever reason, he always chose my yard to do his business in. I was not amused!"

Catching on to what Rex was describing, Donna broke out laughing.

"Anyway," Rex went on to say, "while sitting at my radio shack early one morning, talking on 40 meters, I glanced up just in time to see the dog hike his leg up on my flagpole antenna. First, I saw a bright spark outside my window as the overloads popped on my amplifier, then I saw the dog take off like he had been fired out of a cannon, howling as if from the depths of hell. And the dog's owner had no idea what just happened. All he could do was chase after him, screaming his name. Personally, I don't think the dog slowed down until he hit another zip code."

Donna burst out laughing again as the images of Rex's description started taking shape in her mind. As her laughter subsided, Rex spoke up and said, "Wait, hold on, it gets even better!"

Wiping the laughter tears from her eyes and trying to catch her breath, she begged Rex to stop, as she was now to the point of belly laughing and almost falling out of her chair.

After a few moments, she gave Rex the thumbs-up to go ahead with the rest of the story. As if recalling a children's fairy tale, he began, "About three weeks later, here comes that same man, but this time his dog was on a leash. As they came walking down the sidewalk getting closer to my house, the dog laid down and literally refused to walk past my house. The owner called his name, scolded him, and finally resorted to trying to drag him, but to no avail. After a few minutes of this chaos, he finally gave up, so he turned and walked across the street, and the dog was more than eager to obey. From then on, none of his walks included the sidewalk in front of my house or the use of my yard."

After a few seconds of silence, they both started laughing all over again. Once the storytelling time was over, Rex started pushing buttons, turning dials, and flipping switches.

Donna watched with amazement as he brought this beast to life. "Rex, it only took me a nanosecond to figure out that this set-up is definitely far past a CB radio," she said, "and while I do understand they are radios, what kind are they? This is like nothing I have ever seen before."

With a smile on his face surveying all the lights and dials that had come to life, almost like a mad scientist, Rex replied, "To the world, this is amateur radio, or ham radio—whichever you want to call it—but to me, I still call them my magic boxes."

Leaning back in her chair in amazement, Donna whispered to where only she could hear, "Magic boxes." She wanted to know more.

After listening to Rex, Donna concluded that he was a highly intelligent man, a walking history book on just about any subject that was brought up. Her knowledge of exactly who this man was, was broadening.

Chapter 3

Donna

Donna's mind had prepared to ask the next question, but before she could speak it out loud, voices started coming out of Rex's magic boxes.

It was a man spitting out letters from the alphabet, and numbers as well. Then just as soon as he stopped, another man responded. This man spoke in more letters and numbers. Then both men engaged in a normal conversation, except for the code stuff. Or at least, to Donna, it sounded like some form of code. *Q this, Q that?*

Looking over at Rex with some surprise, she managed to ask him, "Are they talking in code?"

Rex turned away from the radios and shook his head no. "No, ma'am. What you heard was one man calling out the call sign of someone he wanted to talk to, followed by giving his own call sign."

Still a little bit confused, Donna replied, "I get the gist of what you're saying, and at the same time, I don't fully understand. Help a friend out, please."

Rex spoke as if trying to clear the confusion off her face, "Let me give you an example." He continued, "My call sign is W5EAK, and let's say I want to reach out to one of my friends, another veteran friend of mine, Tom, whose call sign is KI5ECE." He paused for a moment as if lost in thought. His gaze went from Donna over to his radios and then back to her. "I'll go one better. Let me just try to reach him." Reaching over to one of the dials, Rex turned it until the number 7.245 MHz showed up on the display. At the same time, he explained that this was a group of sailors on what was called a Navy Net.

"First," he said, "I check for the clear frequency by listening to make sure I don't 'walk on' or 'interfere' with others who may already be talking on the frequency. Next, I step on my PTT switch, which means 'push to talk.' My next step is to speak clearly into the microphone calling out Tom's call sign, KI5ECE, and then I give out my call sign by saying, 'This is W5EAK,' so he will know who is trying to get in touch with him. Most of the time, however, we do recognize each other's voice."

Donna thought watching Rex turn knobs, push buttons, and speak into the microphone looked like a dance in slow motion; it was all so smooth, not to mention something Rex undoubtedly had done many, many times in his life. After no one responded back to his transmission, Rex looked back at Donna.

"Now what?" she asked him.

"Seems Tom is busy elsewhere and not on the radio right now, so I need to clear off this frequency so others can use it," Rex explained.

After clearing off the Net, he turned his office chair back to face Donna as she asked, "What is a Net?"

"Donna," Rex responded, "a Net is like referring to a group of people. Usually, it's a group who have the same interest or hobby. There are Nets for just about anything you can think of, such as veterans of the different branches of service, fishing, quilting, prayer groups, Bible study, YLs, genealogy, storm spotting, storm chasers, song writers, and one time I even heard a bunch of rodeo people talking as they were heading from one rodeo to another. The list goes on and on."

Looking at the radio, Donna said, "I had no idea this world even existed; it sounds like an unbelievable adventure to me. What are YLs?"

"Well," he said, "that is what you would be referred to on the radio. A 'YL' is a lady, no matter her age. An 'OM' is what they call us guys."

Trying hard to curb her laughter, she said, "So, Young Lady and Old Man?"

"Yes, ma'am, that's correct...unless the YL is married; then she is referred to as a XYL. Another important factor about amateur radio is you will never hear the 'seven dirty wordys,' which is code for bad language. Unlike CB radio, anyone holding an amateur radio license is subject to the FCC, meaning the Federal Communications Commission. There are rules to follow, and follow them we must or be in danger of getting fined or reprimanded, with the worse possible scenario being having our licenses revoked. And, oh yes, one more possibility–you could be the winner of a federal paid vacation to prison."

"Ouch," Donna said. "That sounds serious."

"Trust me, Donna, it is," was Rex's response. Continuing with his thought, he went on, "To hold an amateur radio license is a privilege, and there is great responsibility that goes with it, but the flip side of that coin is, it's an amazing adventure with great benefits."

"Rex, I have a question. What do you do when someone doesn't understand your call sign? Just in everyday life, people can mix up or misunderstand letters that sound so much alike, such as 'B' and 'D,' or 'M' and 'N,' etc."

"Good question, and a good catch, by the way," Rex said. "We have a method to prevent that. It's called the phonetic alphabet. Have you ever heard of that before?"

Donna shook her head no, then said, "No, sir, I haven't heard about any of this before. And my curiosity is all over the place right now!"

"I'll give you an example with my call sign," Rex said. "Since I was calling for Tom and he knows my call sign as well as my voice, there usually isn't a problem. However, to give you a demonstration, I could have also said, 'This here is W5EAK–Whiskey 5, Echo, Alpha, Kilo.'"

"Come again? What did you just say?" she asked.

Rex laughed and repeated himself, saying, "Take the first letter of each word, Whiskey 5, Echo, Alpha, Kilo, and you get W5EAK."

The lightbulb finally went off in Donna's head. She responded with, "Oh okay, that makes sense to me now."

Chapter 4

Donna

"How on God's green earth did you ever get into amateur radio, sir?" Donna asked. "Something tells me you didn't just wake up one morning and say, hey, I think I want to be an amateur radio operator!"

Leaning back in his chair laughing, Rex said, "Well, it wasn't exactly like that. If you have time, I would like to share my story with you."

Donna said, "My day is open—no rodeo today—so shoot Luke or lose your guns, sir." She noticed that when she referenced rodeo, Rex's eyes lit up like a kid staring at a wrapped Christmas present sitting under the Christmas tree. Observing the twinkle in his eyes, she thought, *This is quite interesting. I'm gonna file that note away in my little computer brain.* She would save that tidbit of information for a later conversation.

Seeming to come back to reality, Rex asked, "Remember when I called the radios my magic boxes?"

"Yes, I do, and I must admit, it didn't quite make much sense to me until you explained it."

"Donna, most people don't get it. So, sit back and let me tell you a story."

In what seemed like a softer voice as if he were recalling some very precious memories, Rex began sharing his story with Donna, which she felt like he had probably never told anyone before. He took a trip down memory lane.

"Growing up in the 1950s," he began, "me and my friends spent a lot of time down at the movie house. It only cost us a dime for the matinees. My mother would give me a dime as my allowance for doing all my weekly chores without being told to. The ticket for a matinee was nine cents, which left a penny for a piece of candy."

Donna interrupted, asking, "No money for a drink?"

Resuming his story, he replied, "No, we drank from the water fountain. Most of the movies we saw were Westerns and adventure films. By the end of every movie we saw, we all wanted to be cowboys, heroes, and explorers. While there were several adventure movies we all loved, there is one I particularly remember. In this movie, a plane crashed in the Amazon jungle. The passengers and crew survived the crash, but alas, they were hopelessly stranded. One of the passengers was a radio operator from World War II and quickly went to work on the aircraft radio system."

"Wait a minute, wait a minute," Donna said, throwing up her hands to ask for a timeout. "If the crew survived, why didn't they start working on the radio to call for help?"

"Well, the only thing I know to tell you is it wasn't in the script; plus, in this movie they were only pilots. Anyway... back to my story, Donna!"

Donna quickly figured out she had better put the shut to the up if she wanted to hear the rest of it.

"The WWII veteran got the HF/short wave radio to work using parts and wire from the HF, as well as the VHF radio. He set about looking for any parts he could use from the crashed airplane. Taking a generator and a battery from the airplane, he was able to use them by putting a hand crank on the generator and thereby becoming a power source for the radio. Then he made a Morse code key with pieces of metal off the plane. Then he could do this." Rex stopped talking and reached over on the top of his desk. He took his pointer finger and started tapping:

..._ _ _ ...

With a puzzled look, Donna spoke up and said, "Wait, what did you just do?"

With somewhat of a smirk on his face, Rex replied, "I tapped out in Morse code what that man did in the movie: SOS."

"Too cool!" Donna exclaimed. "Way too cool! But hold up. I have to ask, was there any love interests in this movie, or was it all just about a plane crash? My lightning-fast mind tells me if it was only about an airplane crash, that would be too boring."

"Oh yes," he replied, "there was a potential love triangle. There was a girl who really liked one of the pilots, but this pilot was conceited and quite rude to her, as well as everyone else."

"Well, I have to ask, was he conceited as in handsome or an outstanding pilot?"

Pondering her question for a few moments, Rex replied, "To the best of my recollection, in my opinion, it was both!" Then he continued with his story, "So, the girl fell out of 'heavy like' with the pilot and quickly fell in love with the WWII veteran who was saving the day."

With a perplexed look on her face, Donna asked, "Why haven't you said anything about the love story?"

Rex started laughing and said, "Donna, I was 11 years old, and at that time of my life, all girls had cooties! Any more questions?"

"Yes, sir," Donna said. "Was the movie in color or black and white?"

Giving her a look of disapproval and through gritted teeth, Rex said, "It was black and white. And I would like to finish my story before suppertime rolls around if you don't mind!"

"Sorry, Rex, I will try to hold back from interrupting your story. The optimal word here is 'try.' No promises."

Seeing that she had ruffled his feathers somewhat, Donna quickly assumed the position of listening and not talking.

Rex continued, "With his headphones on, the hero continued to tap out 'SOS' on his homemade Morse code key and makeshift radio, along with the airplane's ID number."

Donna was confused again, but she figured it was best not to repeat her earlier methods of interrupting Rex and thought it might be best if she raised her hand like she was back in school.

She guessed this caught Rex off guard, and just like a schoolteacher, he called on her and said, "Let me guess. You either have another question or need to know where the bathroom is, correct?"

"Who was listening to the hero tap out the SOS?" Donna asked.

"I am about to get to that part of the story, Donna, give me a minute," Rex said, then continued, "In this movie, a station somewhere in Brazil heard the call for help. Just one problem: no one knew where the SOS was coming from. Meaning no one knew exactly where the plane had gone down. As a rescue operation was launched, other aircrafts using their direction-finding equipment would coordinate with each other and share data. Once the data was put on a map, it became clear that where all the lines crossed had to be where the plane went down. In other words, X marked the spot. Once they knew where they were located, one airplane dropped supplies to them while another rescue mission went upriver to where they were located to bring them home.

"Once everyone got back to civilization, the pilot decided he really wanted the girl, but she wasn't having any of that. Oh no, she only had eyes for the WWII veteran who had saved the day. And with that, he took her hand as they walked off into the sunset. This was only one of several movies that started my interest in becoming a radio operator. Even the Western movies had a telegraph office with men sending and taking messages by Morse code. With each movie, I realized I wanted to know more."

"Okay, I get it now," Donna said. "But you were 11 years old. How did you get from watching it in the movies to actually hands-on doing it?"

With a big grin on his face and in a robust voice, Rex announced loudly and proudly, "Boy Scouts! By this time of my life, I had already been a Cub Scout and was now a Boy Scout. That's where I discovered there was not an age limit; anyone could become an amateur radio operator if they passed the test. And to put the cherry on top, they offered a merit badge. And to this 11-year-old, that was spiffy!"

Donna giggled and repeated, "Spiffy?"

In a stern voice, Rex quickly responded, "Yes, ma'am, spiffy! Back then, you not only had to pass a written test, but you were required to be proficient in Morse code at so many words a minute. If you were going after a Novice License, your Morse code proficiency rate had to be a minimum of five words a minute. A Tech License also required five words a minute. If you ever decided to step up to a General License, then you were required to do 13 words a minute. Then if you felt froggy and wanted to jump all the way to Extra Class, you had to be able to do Morse code at 20 words a minute. Today, however, you are not required to know Morse code, and it's no longer on the test."

Donna looked down at her cell phone, checking the time. She realized then that she could sit and listen to Rex's stories for hours on end. After seeing how late in the day it was, though, she jumped up, exclaiming, "Oh man, look at the time! I have got to get home and feed Banjo and Moondoggie." Laughing, she added in a loud voice, "Their stomachs probably think their throats have been cut, not to mention I need to get ready for the work week."

"WORK!" Rex exclaimed. "WORK! The horror! That's a bad four-letter word in my vocabulary."

Laughing as they walked to the front door, Donna told Rex that she had thoroughly enjoyed her visit. "Maybe we can pick our conversation back up next weekend?"

Rex agreed, saying that sounded like a good plan, and they would talk later. With a "Goodnight, sir," Donna climbed up in her "Little Red Truck" and headed home.

Just as soon as she pulled into the driveway, her horse, Moondoggie, and Banjo, her Blue Heeler dog, quickly let her know they were a little less than amused that she missed their normal feeding time. As if they could respond to her, Donna looked over at Banjo and told him if he laid down on a slight incline, he would probably roll all the way to the bottom. Then, she turned her attention to Moondoggie and remarked that it wouldn't hurt him to miss a meal or so. "As a matter of fact, you don't exactly walk; it's more like a pregnant woman's waddle. So, let's stop with the evil eye, okay?"

After feeding both of them and giving them a little extra loving, Donna turned off the barn lights and wished them a good night. Heading up to the house, she was ready to put her weary bones to bed. It had been a long, hard week. Time for rest.

Chapter 5

Donna

Heading out to work bright and early the next morning, Donna's mind replayed the conversation and stories Rex shared with her the night before. Her conclusion was that he was one smart dude. To think he had been only 11 years old and was working out in his mind how to be an amateur radio operator…That was amazing.

Donna's sister, Toni, walked in the front door of the office then and saw her laughing. She looked at Donna and asked, "What's so funny?"

Donna composed herself enough to talk to her. "Toni," she replied, "Rex was telling me a story over the weekend, and part of it was that, at the age of 11, he and his friends thought girls had cooties, and I guess it struck me as comical."

Setting file folders down on the edge of her desk, Toni looked back at her and said, "If I remember correctly, at the age of 11, you felt the same way about boys."

"True," Donna said.

This was going to be a very busy week in the house-moving world, as well as the high school rodeo world. However, even with all the irons Donna had in the fire, the buck would stop with her. And taking a chapter out of her Daddy's life, she knew she had to keep pushing. If you get knocked down, get back up. Don't ever give up.

Setting her things down on her desk, Toni and Donna went about gathering up permits, walkie talkies, paperwork, and hard hats and vests, getting ready to leave out on the job. Donna could hear her Daddy and brother, Gary, going over the list of what all they needed for this job. After almost a whole week of loading this big, beautiful, historical house, it was finally moving day.

Leaving the office, their Daddy hollered back at Toni, "Don't forget your camera! This morning I shaved, shampooed, and shined in five minutes, and I am feeling very good-looking today!"

Yes, sir, the day was starting off with a good laugh.

There was never a dull moment with Donna's Daddy, which she attributed to him having such a great outlook on life. Thinking back on some of the ups and downs he had been through, she decided this made him an optimist, as he saw the glass half full. He wasn't a pessimist who saw the glass half empty.

During the move that day, Donna happened to hear the main office calling them on the two-way radio: "Base to T-14, Base to T-14," which was Debbie trying to reach them.

Donna's Daddy heard the office transmitting and grabbed a mic in one of the trucks to respond back, "T-14, go ahead, Base."

After a few transmissions back and forth between him and the office, Debbie cleared off the frequency, saying, "Base clear, KEQ856." This brought back everything Donna had learned from Rex about amateur radio. Obviously, there was much more to this style of radio than met the eye. *Interesting, very interesting,* she thought.

The move itself was going as smoothly as it could. If there had ever been a book on how to move a house, it would say this move was textbook perfect. Coming up on the most difficult portion of the house move, Donna looked over at her brother and Daddy to see them looking back at her. She was watching one side of the house, while Gary was watching the other side. Both of them gave signals back to their dad. All three of them knew they were coming up to one of the tightest places to get a house through that they had ever done. It felt like they were perfectly lined up—now it was time to take a few minutes to breathe and get a drink of water before proceeding forward.

As they waited for the electric company to lift the overhead lines so that they could proceed with moving the house, reporters started coming up to Donna's Daddy, asking him, "H.D. Snow, are you sure this house is going to fit between those two telephone poles that are directly across the street from each other?"

Standing there off to the side, Donna waited to hear what she knew would be a funny one-liner, as this was something her Daddy was known for. And he did not disappoint. Turning to the crowd of reporters, he said, "We use the principle of measure twice, so you only have to cut once. And that, my friends, has never let me down."

"So, Mr. Snow, you are going on record saying this building will fit between those two telephone poles?"

"Son," her Daddy replied to the reporter, "that house will go right between those two telephone poles, slicker than snot on a doorknob!" And once again, H.D. had everyone laughing.

Just as soon as the electric company gave the "all-clear to proceed" signal, everyone was ushered out of the street and back to the sidewalks. Like a well-oiled machine, Donna went back to her side of the house, Gary went to his side of the house, and their Daddy made his way to the front, directing the driver of the pull truck–the 2018 Mack Truck affectionately known as "Thelma."

Watching their respective sides of the house as well as each other and giving hand signals back to their dad, the house went between the telephone poles with literally an inch to spare on each side. With the hardest part of the move behind them, they all breathed a sigh of relief, knowing the rest of the move would be a cake walk.

* * *

By the end of the workday, after the successful moving of the house, everyone seemed to be dragging, tired and sweaty from the scorching Texas summer heat. But all in all, it was a good tired. Putting all the trucks and equipment up was just part of the job at the end of the day, no matter how tired they were. While the men all talked about going home, getting a shower, eating a bite of supper, and settling back and relaxing with some TV for the rest of the evening, Donna knew that she was going home to grab a quick shower, but her day wouldn't end there. She had an important rodeo team meeting that night.

Leaving the yard to head home, Donna pulled up beside her Daddy as he was walking to his pickup and remarked about how close the width of the house was compared to the distance between the telephone poles. "You know, Daddy, we had two inches, only two inches to work with—literally one inch on each side!"

H.D. smiled at her and said, "Donna, in our line of work, two inches is as good as a mile!"

Donna laughed as she waved goodbye and rolled her window up.

* * *

Pulling into the parking lot of the rodeo meeting place, Donna's mind lined up all the things she needed from the backseat of the pickup: computer, rodeo schedule, pen and paper in hand—ready for the meeting.

The meeting went off without a hitch, and as it drew to a close, the Student President asked if anyone had anything else they would like to share with the team. One of the parents raised his hand, waiting to be recognized, and said he wanted to share a story with everyone about an incident he felt they needed to hear.

The Student President yielded the floor for the parent to speak. He made his way to the podium and had everyone's undivided attention. Trying to keep his emotions in check, he began, "Y'all know my son, Cody, who graduated last year and left for college."

It was so quiet in the room, you could have heard a pin drop. Donna wasn't sure what he was about to tell them, but by his trembling voice and body language, she knew it couldn't be good.

"Cody and his best friend were so excited to find out they'd been hired to haul hay for the summer," he went on. "Their motto was, 'You call, we haul. No matter how far.' Well, they got their wish. However, it was a rather lengthy job, and we weren't all that crazy about them being that far away from home. Deep East Texas was their destination to pick up the hay and bring it back here.

"On the long stretch of highway heading back home, they were traveling on a two-lane road through the hills of East Texas. Within a matter of seconds, a large tractor trailer rig—we are told it was a Bull Wagon—passed them going the opposite direction. Due to the excessive speed it was traveling, the authorities believe it created what they described as a wind vortex. This, in turn, pushed the pickup and trailer over to the shoulder of the road, setting them up for a blow-out on the gooseneck trailer with all the hay on it. This caused Cody, who was driving, to lose control of the pickup, as they were whipped around like a wet noodle. The end result was, the pickup and gooseneck trailer ended up on its side."

Gasps could be heard all over the room.

"While they were bruised and shaken up, they were okay," Cody's father continued. You could hear and literally feel the relief as it washed over the room. He went on, "EMTs arrived and made sure the boys were safe. The only other issue was, now all that hay they were hauling was scattered all over the roadside.

"We jumped in our pickups and headed towards them as fast as we could. The most traumatic part of us driving to our sons was the fact that we only had cell phone service for about the first 30 minutes of an approximately four-and-a-half-hour trip."

Donna surveyed the room and noticed that just about every parent was reaching for their youths' hands, no doubt imagining it could easily be their child in this situation. Everyone in that room seemed to know immediately the helplessness you feel when you cannot reach a loved one on the cell phone, or communicate with loved ones.

As Cody's father yielded the floor back to the Student President and walked back towards his seat, you could clearly see tears fall from his eyes, as well as the eyes of everyone in the room.

Leaving the rodeo meeting that night, many thoughts ran through Donna's head.

Chapter 6

Donna

After giving it a lot of thought, Donna decided she wanted to be able to talk to the world like Rex did. She told him as much when she saw him the next day.

She approached him and all but hollered, "You set me up, didn't you? Inviting me over after church every Sunday, showing me which button to push or knob to turn? Introducing me to the ham radio world, whether I am talking or just listening? Letting me talk on the radio to people from all across the United States and some other countries?"

Rex smiled and said, "Did it work?"

Donna laughingly admitted, *it did*. After they finished chuckling, she asked, "Now what?"

Rex replied, "Back to school for you."

"Wait, what? School?" she repeated.

"Don't panic," he said. "It's not as bad as you think it is. As a matter of fact, let's go see my friend, Fast Eddie. His call sign is KD4RAZ. He should be at the Ham Radio Outlet Store, or HRO, as we call it. That's where we can get you the best study book. Then, once you have finished the book, you can take your test."

"Oh man," Donna blurted out, "I thought I was through with school tests!"

With a possum-eating grin on his face, Rex said, "Trust me, Donna. You are getting all wrapped around the axle for no reason at all. Like

I said, you will read through a book. I am always available to answer any technical questions. Then, there are several websites that allow you to take practice tests for free. You can take as many practice tests as you want to; take as many as needed to help you feel confident. Then, when you feel like you are ready, you can get with a ham club administering the test. Once you pass the test, you will file with the FCC, the Federal Communications Commission, for your license, who will in turn issue your call sign. Once that is done, my friend, you are in business, ready to go on the air without my help, care, custody, or control.

"How about next Saturday, you, Ronan, and I head on over to Ham Radio Outlet, and I will introduce you to Eddie? We can buy a book to get you started on this great adventure that, I promise you, you will never regret."

Donna looked at Rex and replied, "Sounds like a plan to me, sir. Since I have rodeo Friday night, which usually runs late, let's not make it too early."

* * *

Bright and early, around lunch the following Saturday morning, Rex, Ronan, and Donna walked through the doors of the Ham Radio Outlet Store.

In a loud voice, she exclaimed, "Oh my gosh, have you ever seen so many radios in one place?" But there was no response to her question. She turned around to find out why Rex hadn't answered her back, and she realized he was standing there staring at every radio on every shelf, much like a kid in a candy store.

"Rex…Rex…Earth to Rex!" she called.

Finally, as if snapping out of a trance, Rex managed, "Oh yes, sorry."

"You need a handkerchief to wipe that drool off your face before we talk to anyone?" she said jokingly. And again, it was as if the lights were on and no one was home. Rex was in his own little world. Donna hadn't realized quite how important radios were to him.

As they approached the counter, there stood a man who Donna figured had to be Eddie, and sure enough, he was.

"Good morning, Eddie," Rex said, taking the lead. "I would like to introduce you to my friend, Donna. We need a book. She wants to study for her Technician's License."

Speaking directly to Donna, Eddie said, "Welcome to our store, Donna. We are glad you're here. And I believe you will find all the study materials over on that far wall. If you have any questions, just let me know."

As Eddie led them both over to the aisle he mentioned, Donna began to have second thoughts about this whole deal. Turning around, she said to Rex, "What if I flunk the test?"

Rex laughed a little under his breath, then became serious. "I believe in you, Donna. Try believing in yourself. And remember, none of us are ever too old to learn."

Taking a moment to think about what Rex had just said, Donna came to the conclusion that he was right; she could do this.

On the way home from the radio store, she started flipping through the book and quickly discovered, to her amazement, it didn't look too bad.

"It really isn't," Rex commented. "And the test, well, it's multiple choice, and like I said, you can take the practice test as many times as you need to feel confident that you are ready for the formal test."

Donna breathed a sigh of relief, watching Rex merge into highway traffic as they headed back to his home. She felt much better about obtaining her license.

* * *

For the next few weeks, every day after work, Donna would religiously read her study book. Rex was right in that it wasn't as bad as she thought. As a matter of fact, she would have already read the whole book had it not been for her full-time job. Once she had read through the book in its entirety, it was time to start taking the practice test.

Every evening after work, upon arriving home, she first took care to feed and water the livestock. Next on the chores list was cleaning out the horses' stalls and finally watering the plants on her back deck. Once all the outside chores had been taken care of, she would head on into the house, fix a small bite to eat, and start studying.

At the end of this particular evening, she had been working on her practice test. Having taken the test 10 times in a row and scoring 100% each time and feeling very pleased with herself, she decided it was time. Time to take the plunge and sign up for the official test. It turned out, signing up wasn't the hard part; the hard part was convincing herself that she was prepared. It was time…No turning back now.

The lead Volunteer Examiner, Sam, and two additional VEs put all her fears at ease. Sam was very kind and obviously could tell she was very nervous. Her Technician's test had 35 questions, of which she could miss up to nine. It turned out, she only missed one question! She passed!

The next step was for Sam to turn her application in to the Federal Communications Commission and await her call sign. What seemed like weeks turned out to be only a few days.

With her call sign in hand, "W5SML," and a trip back to visit Eddie at Ham Radio Outlet to purchase a YAESU FTM400 VHF/UHF analog/digital radio, with dual band antenna for her pickup, she was ready to talk to the world.

Later that afternoon on her way home from work, Donna made contact with Rex, W5EAK, and they talked during her short drive home. It seemed Rex was impressed that she didn't have what the amateur radio world called "mic fright." He went on to explain that even in an area all by yourself with just you and the microphone, some first timers found it hard to speak into the microphone.

Laughing at him, Donna responded back, “Well, we all know I am no stranger to talking, and besides that, I have been talking on the office two-way system for many years.”

“Point taken,” Rex replied.

Chapter 7

Donna

The summer heat was really taking its toll on Donna's flowers across the back deck, with them requiring watering more often than usual. It seemed that tending flowers often helped Donna think things through and work out problems. But what was on her mind wasn't so much a problem as it was trying to figure out the feeling she had been experiencing—what with high school rodeo season starting up, and then this idea of amateur radio. Something deep down in her gut was telling her there was a connection, but she just couldn't quite put her finger on it.

As she pulled some weeds that had sprouted up, it dawned on her that there were many different types of greenery and flowers, and yet they all grew out of the same soil. Surveying her back deck from left to right, there were various green plants as well as blooming plants. Some of the plants didn't return every year, while some came back stronger. And as different as each one was, collectively, they were so pretty. *Very interesting…*

Talking out loud as if the plants could respond back to her, she said, "You know, each of the rodeo kids are unique in their own way, as well as Rex. You have some who are greenery; they mostly blend in. Then you have the cacti; those who are not so pleasant to be around. Next are the blooming flowers, some morning glories, some sweet peas, and let's not forget the snap dragons!"

The conclusion of her talk with the plants was, yes indeed, she needed to make some introductions. Plant a few seeds, water them, and see where it leads. And there was no time like the present to get started.

With the rodeo season starting up, Donna decided she would introduce Rex to the rodeo team, and the rodeo team to Rex. Her thinking was that they could benefit from each other, by either friendship or experience. You know what they say: you are never too old to teach or too young to learn. It all comes down to just paying attention to things going on around you.

After tending to the plants, it was time to feed the stock.

Walking into the house afterwards, she looked at the clock hanging on the living room wall and thought, *Hopefully it isn't too late to call Rex. Even if it is, he can just wake up.* As luck would have it, he was still up.

One ring, two rings.

"Well, howdy," came the voice on the other end of the line.

Donna responded, "Sure hope I'm not interrupting anything."

"Not at all," was Rex's response. "Just getting ready for bed. Since I get up so early in the morning to get on the Nets, as a rule, I hit the sack early."

"Oh good," she replied. "I have a question for you, sir. Or actually, it's more like an invitation."

"Well, my friend," he said, "you have my full attention. What's on your mind?"

"Been doing a lot of thinking," she told him, "about our talks regarding radios, and life in general. After putting considerable thought into it, I believe you and the rodeo team would be a good fit. Would you be interested in attending a meeting and seeing if you agree?"

After a few seconds of silence on the other end of the phone, Rex finally spoke up and said, "Donna, I'm not sure what I could offer, but I am open to anything that helps youth."

"Good, I was hoping you would say that!" she exclaimed, trying to hide her excitement. "It's settled. Our next meeting is this coming Monday night. Later tonight, I will text you all the details of the location and time."

Rex responded with, "Sounds good to me. See y'all then."

With that, Donna hung up the phone, mighty pleased with herself.

* * *

The following Monday, as everyone was arriving for the rodeo meeting, there was Rex pulling in, too. It was hard to miss his Suburban, as it stuck out like a sore thumb with the humongous antenna on the front. Donna thought the kids looked like they were sizing him up.

It was easy to see, because of Rex's license plate with the Bronze Star and "Disabled American Veteran" printed on it, that he had served in the military. The kids probably didn't understand why he was there; their curiosity was surely rising. This curiosity was exactly what Donna was hoping for.

Rex walked towards the fire pit where the meeting was being held. There was a sea of cowboy hats visiting with each other until the meeting was called to order. It was 7:00 p.m. on the dot when Amelia, the Student President, began the meeting. After an opening prayer, Amelia asked Greg to take roll call.

Setting his notebook on a bale of hay, which acted as the podium, Greg started calling out names.

"Amelia…"

"Here."

"Amy…"

"Here."

"Ariel…"

"Here."

"Brady…"

"Here."

"Bubba…"

"Here."

"Houston…"

"Here."

"Madison..."

"Here."

"Middle P..."

"Here."

After everyone answered the roll call, Greg yielded the floor back to Amelia.

While the meeting proceeded on with its usual reports, Rex leaned over to Donna and asked, "What's with that young lady, Madison? I could barely hear her."

Donna whispered back, "Yes, I know. She is the epitome of a wall-flower. She does her best to blend into the woodwork, and everyone knows you have to strain your ears to even hear her talk. Madison is a freshman, and her parents are hoping we can draw her out of her shell."

"Oh, I see," Rex responded.

Donna went on to describe the rest of the rodeo team to her guest: "Amelia and Amy are twins, in case you haven't figured it out."

Laughing under his breath, Rex responded, "Well to be honest, before the meeting started, I did think I was seeing double."

After a small but quiet giggle between them, Donna continued, "There's Greg, the youth secretary who always seems so serious, but I think that's because he's highly intelligent. Then you have Houston; he's the red-headed, freckle-faced kid who is always smiling, sitting over there to the right of the podium. Next to Houston is Bubba. Now, that young man is what my grandmother would call a tall drink of water—very tall and skinny. I honestly believe that when Bubba is fully grown... Well, let's just say I wouldn't want to make him mad."

Turning to the other side of the room, she pointed to Brady next. "Brady is a calf roper, and he really wants to go pro someday. Always makes great grades in school, committed to working out and practicing. You already know who Madison is. Most of the time, you can't hear her, because her long black hair blocks most of her face, making it hard to even read her lips. Last but not least, we have Ariel, a very sweet, kindhearted young lady who has a heart to help anyone, anytime. And I assure you, she is one of the hardest working young ladies you will ever meet."

After listening to Donna go down the list of all the rodeo kids, Rex looked at her and said, "You speak of each one as if they were your own child."

With a little bit of a grin on her face, she answered him back, "Yes, sir. Some days, I want to hug them to pieces, and some days I just want to whip their legs!"

* * *

At the appropriate time during the meeting, Donna raised her hand to be recognized by the Youth Board President and was given the floor. Speaking loudly, she turned to the crowd of parents and kids, saying, "I would like to introduce my guest, Lieutenant Commander E.A. King III, United States Navy Retired, along with his service dog, Ronan."

As Rex stood up, everyone applauded, welcoming their guest and thanking him for his service. Rex said, "Just call me Rex."

One of the kids asked, "Why do they call you Rex? Your first name starts with an E."

Laughingly, he replied, "Since no one could ever pronounce my Irish first name correctly, my grandmother gave me the nickname of Rex, which is Latin for King."

Speaking up from the back of the group, Houston said, "So does that make your name King-King?" Everyone, including Rex, got a good laugh out of that one.

Rex watched intently as the rodeo kids conducted their meeting, mostly by Robert's Rules of Order. You could tell the returning team members from the new ones by the way they participated in the meeting.

One of the agenda items was their hosted rodeo that was coming up. It was time for each parent and rodeo team member to sign up for which area of the rodeo they wanted to work. As a rule, the moms worked the concession stand, and the dads handled areas in the arena. As the Adult Board President, Christopher, was going down the work list, each team member would raise their hand, waiting to be called on to get their favorite job at the rodeo. This hosted rodeo was an "all hands on deck" event, and the rodeo team members and their parents all knew this was their main way to raise money for their outings, as well as the end-of-year awards banquet.

Once the meeting was adjourned, some of the kids saddled their horses to practice in the arena, while others headed over to the fire pit to hang out with their friends.

Donna walked over to Rex with the intention of asking him what he thought about the meeting. But before she could say a word, Rex spoke up, saying, "Donna, this is an awesome group of kids. They ran their meeting, discussed the financial report, and went through all the committee reports. I am more than impressed; I am almost speechless. Had no idea there was rodeo teams in school. Up in Wichita County, where I grew up, we did have high school rodeos, but not as organized as this."

"Well," she responded, "rodeo is not recognized by the school as University Interscholastic League—UIL—so we do it separate from the school, most often with their blessing. They like the idea that there is something offered to each child."

She went on to describe, "You have the football team, the baseball team, the soccer team, the chess club, the debate club, the cheerleaders, shop club, library club... You would think that would cover every young person at school. Sadly, it doesn't. Back in the beginning, 1972, it seems there were a few boys that just didn't fit in anywhere, and well, let's just say they were trouble with a capital 'T.'

"The leadership of the schoolboard recognized there was a need, yet they didn't know how to fill it. That is, until a few of the parents got together with them, and the next thing you know, the local high school rodeo association was born. The main reason a high school rodeo association was started was to deal with troubled boys. Just like one of the founders said, there isn't nothing like a 2,000-pound bull to straighten out the attitude of a 110-pound boy. Yes, sir, it works every time.

"Their thinking was, this way, young boys would have an option to belong to something. They also hoped these young men would see the error of their ways and start turning their lives around. When asked by the school district what they would get out of this, they all responded the same: 'Knowing we made a difference in these boys' lives is thanks enough.' Realizing there were some students who were 'horse people' and competed as such, the idea of the local high school rodeo team started blossoming into what we have today."

Speaking up, Rex asked, "So all the kids I saw here at the meeting tonight rodeo?"

"Well," she replied, "during their high school years, they rodeo, and some will go on to rodeo after high school, like college, and a few go on to make a living from it by going professional. But most of these kids only rodeo these four years of high school. However, the one thing that never goes away is the friendships they build—not to mention the life lessons they learn."

"Life lessons," Rex muttered under his breath.

Donna went on to explain, "So far, we have had a tire changing clinic. This turned out great, as I didn't realize so many young men didn't know how to change a tire. Really cute story: I was running late from the office one afternoon, and one of the rodeo dads was conducting the clinic here at my house. Pulling into the driveway around the back of the house by the arena, I looked over at one of the girls jumping up and down, clapping her hands. Getting out of my truck and walking over to her, I said, 'Amy, you look excited. Did you learn to change a tire today?'

"She said, 'Oh no, Miss Donna, it's so much better than that. I can open the hood of my car now all by myself.' Seeing the excitement on her face, I started celebrating with her. We have also had an etiquette class. That was something to see! We aren't saying parents don't teach their kids. We are saying that, many times, a kid will listen to a total stranger before they listen to their parents."

Nodding his head in an affirmative way, Rex said, "Good job. I am impressed."

With that, Donna excused herself. "Make yourself at home, and stay as long as you want to. I need to go assist the kids in the arena practicing."

And with that, Donna made her way to the arena. She noticed Rex and Ronan walking over to the fire pit. About 30 minutes later, she stood over by the arena gates, and she could see Rex and Ronan approaching her from her peripheral vision. She asked him, "Did you enjoy the rodeo meeting, sir?"

"Donna, I like what I hear, and I like what I see. Would it be possible for me to attend another meeting?" Rex asked.

Taking a big breath of relief, she replied, "Absolutely, and as a matter of fact, why don't you come to our hosted rodeo coming up? As our guest, of course."

Smiling back at her, Rex said, "I would like that, thank you."

As they watched the kids in the arena practice, Donna decided to share the story from the last meeting about the horrible wreck a couple of the alumni youth had been involved in. Listening intently to every word, she could see Rex's facial expression change from a smile to a frown.

"What a scary time for not only the kids, but also their parents…not being able to keep in contact with them on the road and trying to find them," he said.

"I totally agree with you, sir. I totally agree," she replied.

As Rex opened the back door, giving Ronan the command "up" for Ronan to get into the SUV, Rex turned to Donna and said, "You know, when all else fails, amateur radio still works. Too bad they weren't licensed amateur radio operators."

Waving goodbye to Rex and Ronan, it suddenly clicked for Donna.

That's it! That's what the gut feeling was about…Here is the connection!

Chapter 8

Rex

Driving home, Rex replayed the evening's event in his mind, specifically when he talked with the young men around the fire pit, as it reminded him a whole lot of his life back in Wichita County during his youth.

Rex recalled the events of just an hour ago, when he walked over to the young men, spoke up, and asked if he could sit with them...

Pushing his short, curly red hair under his hat and behind his ears, Houston was the first one to respond to Rex's query.

"Yes, sir, Mr. Rex, have a seat," he said.

Feeling like he was being welcomed into their circle, Rex asked each of them about what events they competed in. One by one, they were more than glad to talk about rodeo. After each youth took his turn, Houston spoke up, asking Rex, "Sir, did you ever rodeo?"

Looking up from the fire, Rex smiled and said, "Why, yes I did." It was easy to see he had piqued their interest and now had their undivided attention. "Growing up around livestock," he continued, "well, I guess it just gets down in your blood." Looking into the face of each of the young men, Rex grinned and went on, "Let me share a funny story with you."

The boys were hanging onto every word he said. Rex thoroughly enjoyed taking a trip down memory lane, as he was transported back to his youth and rodeo days.

"Not sure if y'all can identify with me, but I was trying to impress a girl by getting into bull riding," Rex admitted. "Do y'all know what I mean?"

Every boy there was in agreeance, which they showed by either nodding their head yes or verbally agreeing. Brady said, "Mr. Rex, aren't you a little bit too tall to ride bulls?"

Chuckling, Rex replied, "Yes, sir, too tall. However, I was willing to try just about anything to get this girl's attention so I could ask her on a date. There was a dance after the rodeo, and I wanted her to go with me. I guess you could say I was shy back then, like most boys at that age, and figured I could impress her if I rode a bull.

"All my friends told me I was stupid, as I was too tall to ride bulls, but that didn't stop me. When they saw that I wasn't going to listen to them, they all started trying to help me. Then they went to giving me all sorts of information. One friend told me, 'Rex, watch this bull. Just as soon as he comes out of the chute, he's gonna spin to the right,' and then someone else said, 'No, he spins to the left.' I was a mess of nerves, and most likely the bull picked up on it.

"When the gate opened, out we went, and the dance was on. It seemed like an eternity, but it was, in actuality, around four seconds. This bull bucked and bucked, switching back from left to right and right to left. And about the time he switched back again, he shot me off his back like a cannon, and I saw miles and miles of Texas. When I finally hit the ground, all the air had been knocked out of me. All of a sudden, everyone was screaming, 'Run, Rex, run!' Before my eyes came back into focus, I could see both of those bulls were running right at me."

Bubba started laughing, "Both of those bulls?"

Rex smirked and said, "At that time, there was two of everything. Anyway, I guess self-preservation kicked in, and I started running for the fence. This is when having long legs paid off. I cleared that fence faster than a minnow could swim a dipper! Just as I cleared the fence, the bull slammed into it. It was a close call."

"What happened then, Mr. Rex?" Bubba asked.

"Well, son, I looked up just in time to see my best friend walking hand in hand with the girl I was trying to impress! All in all, the only thing I took with

me from that rodeo was bumps, a lot of bruises, not to mention a bruised ego, and no date for the dance."

Looking over at Rex, Houston said, "I think I can speak for everyone here when I say that we all identify with what you went through–which makes me wonder if girls are even worth the trouble."

Rex responded back with a grin, "Yes, son, it is worth it...with the right girl."

"Mr. Rex," Houston continued, "Miss Donna said you are an amateur radio operator? Can you tell us about that, sir?"

"Oh, I guess I was around 11 years old, and a boy scout, by the way. I learned there was a merit badge for radio, and I wanted that badge more than anything then. First, I got my license, then it was time for a radio. On a limited budget, I went to the Army Navy Surplus stores, where you could get old WWII radios for very little money. They could be modified to work in the amateur radio bands. So, I saved up for one of the radios and all the tubes I needed. With the help of others already licensed, I learned how to make all the old gear work again. It was awesome to see the radios come to life and hear voices from far-off lands in my room. I now had a license, working radios, and 'homebrew' wire antennas hung in the trees. Now I needed to design and print my own QSL card."

All the boys looked at Rex with puzzled faces. Rex then told them how every ham radio wants written proof of contact with far-off stations.

"Since the beginning of ham radio, hams would send postcards acknowledging contact with a station," he said. "In return, that station would send a postcard back, thus proving to both that the contact was made on a certain date, time, frequency, and what gear and antenna was used, etc. The 'QSL' is from the Morse code Q-signals for written confirmation or acknowledgement. There is a bunch of Q-signals, boys. If you ever decide you want to learn Morse code, I will get you a list. The Q-signals allow people to communicate on ham radio without speaking the same language. If y'all learned the Q-signals, you could have your own secret language. That might be neat!"

All the boys were looking at Rex with the most confused expressions. Rex decided it would be beneficial if he gave them a few examples. Such as...

QRA = What is your call sign?
QRV = Are you ready?
QRL = Are you busy?
QSP = I will relay.
QSL = Acknowledged.
QSY = Please change frequency.
QTH = My location.

"Almost like a secret code," Rex went on. "The odds of anyone understanding are slim to none—that is, of course, unless they're an amateur radio operator.

"The tubes on my radio gave off a soft glow through the perforated backing and onto the wall. Listening to people talk on my radio was like hearing word pictures. They would describe where they lived, their culture, such as food, terrain, and customs, and I in turn would describe where I lived. It was because of this adventure that I called them my 'magic boxes.' Guess you could say, at that age, I was a world traveler without leaving my house. I even had a world map on my bedroom wall with a push pin for every place around the world that I had made contact with."

"What did your mother say about all the pin holes you put in the wall?" asked Houston.

"Well, my mother told me when the day came that I moved out of the house, I had to spackle and paint my bedroom all by myself."

Everyone laughed at that, including Rex.

Pulling into his driveway Rex looked over at Ronan and remarked, "Ronan, my friend, it feels like déjà vu from my rodeo days. I think we have found a new purpose, a place where we can be of help. What do you think?"

And as if he had understood every word Rex had spoken, Ronan started barking and wagging his tail.

"As a matter of fact, Ronan, I think I better give Donna a call and get this ball rolling on my idea," Rex said.

Reaching up on the display screen in his SUV, Rex called Donna. Just as soon as she said, "Hello," Rex said, "I would like to ask a favor, Donna. May I talk to the rodeo team and their parents about amateur radio at the next rodeo meeting? You know, like all the perks of being an amateur radio operator—not to mention the fun."

Donna responded, "Sir, it doesn't take me long to look at a hot horseshoe, so the answer is yes, I think that is a great idea. The adult board is always looking for things not only connected to rodeo, but also things outside of rodeo, and I believe this fits the bill. Thank you."

Donna had no way of knowing the impact this new hobby would have, but she was about to find out.

* * *

One evening, during what Rex knew would be a practice night at the arena, he had decided to bring a friend over to introduce to the rodeo team.

Walking over to the roping chute, Rex said, "Hey there, boys. I would like to introduce my friend and fellow amateur radio operator, Sam, otherwise known as NM5N. We are both members of the Cowtown Amateur Radio Club, whose call sign is K5COW."

All the kids spoke up, saying hi to Sam as they finished loading the steers for the evening practice. Bubba asked Sam if he had competed in rodeo before, to which Sam admitted he hadn't.

Rex said, "The reason I asked Sam over was to talk to y'all about amateur radio and all the perks that go with being a licensed amateur radio operator."

"Perks?" Bubba asked.

Taking this as his cue, Sam responded, "Oh yes, sir, there are a few perks most people don't even know about…like you can apply for scholarships every quarter until you earn your undergraduate degree. If you ever decided to join the military, you may be eligible for an advanced pay grade. You could be a certified storm spotter, not to mention that when cell phones go down, ham radio is still there. And...it's fun."

Sam asked if anyone there had ever talked on an amateur radio before. Looking around to see if anyone held up their hand, to everyone's surprise, Greg raised his right hand while his left hand pushed his glasses back up on the bridge of his nose. Greg could immediately tell they were all shocked. One of the team members spoke up and asked him why he hadn't said something before now.

Greg responded back, "I didn't fit in with any team at school, and to be honest, I was beginning to think I didn't fit in with any extracurricular team outside of school. That is, until I met this rodeo team. Y'all treated me like family right from the start, and I was afraid you wouldn't like me if you knew I was somewhat of a geek."

"Are you kidding me?" Houston shouted after looking around at the other team members. "We think it's great!"

"Would you help us as we study to get our licenses?" Bubba asked.

"You bet I will. I'd be glad to!" Greg blurted out.

Looking over at Rex, who was smiling, Sam said, "I bet I can help get everyone—even your parents—licensed within a month."

Laughing out loud, Houston asked, "And what if you can't get us licensed, then what?"

Sam said, "Well, not to worry. I haven't lost a student yet."

Everyone laughed and told Sam he had a deal.

As Houston put the wrap on the next steer in line, he asked Sam, "What do we have to do, and how long will this take, sir?"

Sam responded back, "About 10 hours of your time, plus the test, which is about 30 minutes or less. It's really not hard at all, if you apply yourself. And no worries; it won't interfere with rodeo. Greg said he would help, and I am here to help as well. If everyone is on board, we can start this week."

Each of the boys looked at each other and all at once hollered, "We're in!"

* * *

Over the next three weeks, Sam, in his capacity as a VE (Volunteer Examiner), met up with the rodeo team and many of their parents down at the No Gotty arena. After the last class was over and everyone got ready to take the test, Sam and Rex had every confidence that the students, young and older, would do great.

And they did. All of Sam's students passed!

With the test behind them, everyone seemed to breathe a sigh of relief knowing they had done well. Sam looked at his "rodeo class" and said, "Now, see, that didn't hurt. Just like I said, I haven't lost a student yet."

* * *

Pulling up to the arena on practice night, Sam and Rex decided to surprise the rodeo team with a pizza party in celebration of their accomplishment of becoming amateur radio operators. Sam and Rex had become a part of their rodeo family and often came out to watch their practices. However, on this night, the rodeo team was confused by all the food Sam and Rex were carrying. Walking over to the main arena gate, Houston asked what the pizza was for.

Sam said, "We are celebrating everyone passing their test."

"Awesomeness!" yelled Bubba. "I love pizza, no matter what the occasion is for!"

Putting three slices of pizza on his paper plate, Bubba asked Sam, "Sir, when do we know what our call signs are gonna be?"

Sam responded, "Didn't you know you can go online to fcc.gov and look it up?"

"What?!" Bubba exclaimed. "You mean we can find out now?"

"Yes, sir, you sure can," Sam said as he took his next bite of pizza. "Let me get my laptop out of the pickup, and we can look them up if you want."

Chewing on his last bite, Sam walked over and got his laptop out of his truck. Quickly doing a search, he was able to locate the call signs everyone was waiting for.

"Okay, let's see here…First is Houston. You are Q5JEQ. Bubba, you are Q5OWC. Brady, your call sign is Q5BAD, and Ariel, you are Q5ZKP. Of course, Greg is still Q5AGN."

Rex and Sam had never seen anyone as excited as these kids getting their call signs.

Looking over at Brady, Houston said, "I guess I never realized your middle name started with an A. That makes your initials spell out B-A-D. That's pretty cool!"

Not one to let it go, Ariel was next to speak. She asked Brady, "Does that stand for Allen or Alex?" With a sheepish grin on his face, Brady shook his head no. "Okay, then what does it stand for?"

"If I tell you, promise not to laugh," Brady replied.

"We won't laugh, we promise," was the collected response.

"Actually, I was named after my Grandpa Dalton," Brady said, "and his middle name was Aloysius."

It seemed that it wasn't as easy not to giggle as they had promised. Brady's face was turning red with embarrassment when Greg spoke up and said, "Hey, y'all, Aloysius stands for 'famous warrior'—a wise warrior. Don't think it's a good idea to laugh. If a fight breaks out, we will definitely want him on our side!"

Leaning over, Rex quietly said, "Sam, this is good. Now a younger generation has been bit by the bug, and our hobby will continue on."

Feeling mighty pleased with themselves, they both sat back, propping their boots up on the bottom rung of the arena as they ate pizza and watched the kids practice.

* * *

As days turned into weeks, the rodeo team became more of a family. Brady was consistently shaving hundredths of a second off his roping times. All the practice the kids had been putting in was paying off. Even Madison's goat tying runs were getting smoother and faster. She started hollering, even though no one could hear her except for the Field Judge that was standing less than 10 feet from her. Progress was progress; her times were getting faster, and her voice was getting a little louder.

One of the best things to happen was that so many of them, as well as their parents, got their "ticket," as they had learned to call their amateur radio licenses. These radios had saved their bacon on many occasions. It was a way to communicate with each other—not to mention it was just flat out fun, like Sam had told them!

* * *

In the car, Rex and his longtime friend Doc were driving around town. Looking over at Doc, Rex asked, "Do you mind if we take a few minutes and run by the arena over at Donna's house before we head back?"

"You're driving, I'm riding. Sounds good to me," Doc answered.

Pulling into Donna's driveway, Rex and Doc saw several pickups and jeeps parked in front of an arena. Doc asked his friend, "What is all this?"

"It's a high school rodeo team, and I would like to introduce you to them," Rex replied.

Doc smiled and said, "I love it!"

As they walked over to the arena, most of the kids looked up to see who had just arrived. Bubba said, "Here's Mr. Rex, but I don't recognize the man with him."

"Good evening," Rex said. "We were on our way back from a function over at the National Medal of Honor Museum, and I wanted to introduce the team to my friend, Doc."

One by one, each member of the rodeo team welcomed Doc to practice night.

"We are gonna sit over here and watch y'all practice, then we will meet over at the fire pit," Rex said.

Shaking their heads in acknowledgement, the kids began practice.

"While the kids do that, let's sit down over at the fire pit and visit, Doc. Does that sound okay?"

Doc replied, "Sounds like a good plan to me, Rex."

A short time later, after practice was over and the steers had been fed, the rodeo team made their way to the fire pit, where Rex and Doc had been sitting and visiting. Houston was the first one to speak, asking how Doc knew Mr. Rex.

"Well," Rex replied, "I have known Doc for 40-plus years. Actually, we are both Vietnam Combat Veterans." With half a smile on his face, he continued, "We had both been in the same hospital from wounds we received in Vietnam. As a matter of fact, his proper name is Colonel Don Ballard, U.S. Army RET. He began his military career in the Navy when he was assigned to the Marines as a Hospital Corpsman. After Vietnam, he transferred to the Army National Guard, and all his friends call him 'Doc.'"

Looking around the fire pit at the kids, Doc said with a big smile, "So, y'all had better just call me Doc."

"At the time," Rex went on, "Doc was a Navy Hospital Corpsman, and his heroic actions with the Marines earned him a Medal of Honor."

"What is a Medal of Honor, Mr. Rex?" Ariel asked.

"Well, Ariel, it means that during battle while Doc was helping wounded Marines as they were under heavy fire, an enemy soldier suddenly left his concealed position and, after hurling a hand grenade which landed near the wounded, and after he started firing on the small group of men, Doc fearlessly threw himself upon the lethal explosive device to protect his comrades from the deadly blast. He flung the grenade away, and in the air, it detonated. Then, Doc got up and continued treating other casualties. His heroic actions and selfless concern for the welfare of his companions served to inspire all who observed him and prevented possible injury or death to his fellow Marines."

Looking around at the team and realizing they were literally hanging onto every word he said, Rex paused for a few seconds, then continued, "The Medal of Honor is the highest military honor our country can bestow. As of now, he is one of only 61 living Medal of Honor recipients. Actually, you are in an elite group, as only 0.0000018% of the population will ever meet a living Medal of Honor recipient."

As Doc reached gently into his coat pocket, he pulled out his medal and put it around his neck. The only sound that could be heard was the crackling of the fire; not a word was spoken. The team stared in awe at this national treasure as the flames reflected off his medal, which hung on a blue ribbon.

The evening progressed with all sorts of questions being asked from the kids and Doc alike. It was as if two generations, separated by years, were coming together. With each question Doc answered, the rodeo team gained knowledge about this man and his life. And it was nothing short of amazing.

Bubba asked, "Doc, sir, do you have an amateur radio license like Mr. Rex?"

"No, son, I don't," Doc responded and went on to say, "I'm probably a little too long in the tooth." Realizing this must be a saying the kids had never heard before, which he detected by the confused looks on their faces, he spoke up again and said, "What I am trying to say is this: I am too old. As a matter of fact, I am older than Mr. Rex."

Quickly speaking up, Bubba said, "That radio, sir, doesn't care how old or young you are. Like Miss Donna told us, you are never too young or old to learn. And Doc, if she were here and heard you talking like that, I bet you she would tell you the exact same thing."

Houston joined in on the conversation and said, "And if you disobey, you might end up getting your legs whipped!"

Looking over at Rex, Doc said, "Well, looks like they got me. To be honest, I have often thought about getting my license, so maybe I should look into this. What do you think, Rex?"

"Sounds like you have another adventure coming up, my friend," Rex exclaimed.

As his watch notified him of the late hour, Rex spoke up and said, "Would you look at the time…I better get you back to your hotel, Doc."

Looking around the fire, Doc stared into each of the kids' eyes and thanked them for welcoming an old veteran and making him feel right at home. Shaking each of their hands and saying goodbye, Doc said, "I hope to see each and every one of you again someday. Thank you for letting me be a part of your evening. It was an honor to meet you."

The kids were at a loss for words and all waved goodbye to their new friend—Doc Ballard, a man they would never forget for the rest of their lives.

Chapter 9

Benjamin

Sitting in the front office of his new school, Benjamin, a lonely, dark-haired 15-year-old boy of small stature, was trying to remember just how many different schools he had attended and quickly realized it was too many to count. New foster parents, a new school, new set of bullies, and no friends.

As far as he was concerned, it was all the same song—just the 100th verse. His mind couldn't help but reflect on the last family he had been put with; they were only in it for the monthly income they received from the state. So much per child per month. Lots of money, yet Benjamin and all the other foster kids shared bedrooms and clothes.

Being the oldest foster child in the house, Benjamin had developed a sense of responsibility for the younger kids. The foster dad was a real jerk, and the foster mom, well, she was only as nice as her husband allowed. It was very clear to Benjamin that fostering kids was just a business to the Pruitts. However, he felt like there was more to the story. It was almost like the kids lived on welfare, and the foster parents lived high on the hog.

Oddly enough, Benjamin and his foster siblings looked forward to Mondays since they could all escape to school. It was the weekends they dreaded. Instead of looking forward to running and playing outside, the only thing they had to look forward to was staying in their rooms and playing video games with all the curtains closed. It felt more like a prison than a home. No one to talk to; no one that could help. In a house full of kids, foster parents, and "uncles," Benjamin still felt so alone.

Then, precisely at 8 p.m. every night, it was lights out for all the kids, even Benjamin. Some of his foster siblings had learned the hard way that life would be easier on them if they didn't disobey the "lights out" rule, as the punishment could be severe.

Late one Friday night, lying in bed, Benjamin's curiosity began to get the best of him and finally won. Just like clockwork, there were lights coming through the side of the window, reflecting on his bedroom wall. Slipping out of bed, Benjamin was careful to crawl over to the window, praying that his body weight did not cause the old wooden floor to creak. Slightly pulling the side of the curtain back, he could see headlights as an engine turned off.

Wait a minute, he thought to himself. *No big deal; that's only Uncle Gus.* So, figuring there wasn't anything more to look at, he went back to bed.

Benjamin's world, as well as the world of all the other foster kids, was turned upside down the following Monday as they prepared to leave for school. As usual, their foster mom didn't feed them breakfast, nor did she pack them a lunch. She often told them, "It's the state's responsibility to feed you at school." Heading to the bus, like every other school day, Benjamin and his foster siblings were hoping to get there in time to run by the cafeteria before class.

Stepping up and boarding the bus, Benjamin realized something was very different today. Where were all the other kids that normally rode their bus? When the bus finally came to a stop and the door opened, a familiar face stepped on. Seeing it was Ms. Roberts, their case worker, they all breathed a sigh of relief. It seemed the nightmare they had all been living in was coming to an end.

Benjamin was so glad when he and the other kids were placed elsewhere. Apparently, their foster dad had a side gig of selling drugs, and the kids they took in were just a cover-up. The foster dad and mom were arrested. The "uncles," as the kids were told to call them, got away.

Thinking back on all the foster homes he had been put in, this one was by far the worst. Now that nightmare could be filed away as just a bad memory.

So far, with the Richards, things seemed normal—at least, Benjamin thought so. Walter worked so hard on the family farm, and Benjamin could tell he took pride in his job. His new foster mom, Anne, worked at the local bank as the head teller. While everything seemed normal, Benjamin was waiting for the other shoe to drop, waiting for the "abnormal" to come out…But so far, it hadn't. Definitely a far cry from where he lived before.

The Pruitts wouldn't allow anyone to have a pet—no dog, cat, hamster, not even a parakeet. Nothing. In Benjamin's estimation, it was unfair, because the foster dad had a dog; a pit bull, to be exact.

Even though this was behind Benjamin now, the memories remained.

After what seemed like an eternity staring down at the floor, he heard his name being called. Looking up, there stood a tall, slender, red-headed woman standing in front of him and smiling.

"Welcome, Benjamin," she said. "We are glad you're here. I'm Mrs. Horne, your school counselor. Please follow me to my office. Let's talk, shall we?"

Sitting down in Mrs. Horne's office, Benjamin couldn't help but look around at her unique decor. "Wow!" he exclaimed. "Your office is so different from any other I've seen."

She smiled and said, "Well, Benjamin, my office represents one of my loves: the Western and rodeo world. As a matter of fact, I grew up in this school district and was part of the high school rodeo team."

Looking at the many pictures that sat on her desk and shelves, Benjamin said, "Is this you riding a bull?"

"Yes, it is," she said. "That was back when girls were allowed to ride bulls at the high school level. Sadly, now they don't allow it. Then, when I married and had children, they were introduced to the same world, a world we all love."

Benjamin was a little perplexed. He replied, "Mrs. Horne, I didn't see a 'rodeo team' on the list of school activities."

"Well, Benjamin," she said, "that's because it isn't a UIL sport, meaning it is not supported by the school district. However, here in Texas, you will find that just about every school recognizes rodeo as a huge part of our lives, thereby endorsing it as something that is good for the students who don't feel like they fit into any other school activities." She paused. "Anyway, that's enough about rodeo. Let's get back to you. We need to discuss your classes and walk you around campus. Looks like all your paperwork is in order."

After a few moments of looking through everything, Mrs. Horne said, "I see here that you are a part of the foster system and are currently living with Walter and Anne Richards. I know the Richards family, and I can assure you they are really good people, well established in the community, and I think you will be happy there. That is, if you give it half a chance."

Benjamin sat there, minding his manners, and thought to himself, *I pray you are right, Mrs. Horne. I pray you are right.*

"Last bit of instruction, Benjamin," she went on to say. "If you have any questions about where to go or what to do, all you have to do is ask. That's my job."

* * *

As Benjamin walked around and up and down the hallways of campus, everything seemed easy to remember. It wasn't the smallest or the largest school campus he had been on, but something about it felt different. Benjamin couldn't put his finger on it, but there was an undeniable feeling of peace here. Maybe it was Mrs. Horne, his new teachers, or even some of the kids who actually went out of their way to welcome him to the school. He thought maybe things were turning around, but at the same time, he didn't dare get his expectations too high.

After his last class of the day, when the dismissal bell rang, Benjamin gathered his things and headed out the front entrance when he heard a voice calling his name. Turning around, there stood freckle-faced Houston, a boy he had just met in his last class. Benjamin looked around to make sure Houston was talking to him and not someone else. Feeling reasonably sure Houston was talking to him, Benjamin stopped so the boy could catch up.

"Hey there," Houston said. "Do you want to come hang out at the arena this afternoon?"

"Arena?" Benjamin responded quizzically.

"Heck yeah," Houston said. "I have a small arena behind my house, and we practice chute dogging two times a week—that is, depending on the weather."

"Chute dogging?" Benjamin asked.

Houston laughed. "Again with the questions? Yes, sir, chute dogging. It's fun. You can even give it a try if you want to."

That's when it dawned on Benjamin; he had a made a friend. "Uh, yeah, I guess, but I have to ask my mom, or should I say, foster mom."

"Okay, let's go ask," was Houston's reply.

* * *

As Benjamin and Houston got in the pick-up line, Benjamin saw Anne's car. The two boys ran to greet her.

Rolling the window down, Anne said hello and asked who Benjamin's friend was.

Taking his hat off, Houston said, "Howdy, ma'am. My name is Houston, and it's nice to meet you."

"It's nice to meet you too, Houston," Anne replied.

Houston continued, "Benjamin and I have history class together. Thought I would invite him over to meet some of the other guys from the rodeo team."

Anne seemed happy and delighted to hear this, Benjamin thought.

"Well, Houston," Anne asked, "where do you live?"

Houston said he lived over on Sherwood Drive.

"That's not far from our place," Anne said. "Sure, he can go. What time do y'all start?"

Houston responded, "I can text Benjamin my address and all the details if that is okay, ma'am?"

Looking over at Benjamin, Anne asked if he had any homework. Benjamin was quick to tell her, "No, ma'am, not tonight."

"Okay, then let's get to the house, you take care of your chores, grab a bite of supper, and we will head on over to your house, Houston."

Turning to walk off, Houston hollered out, "It was a pleasure to meet you, ma'am, and Benjamin, I'll see you later tonight, my friend!"

Staring out the passenger window as they headed home, Benjamin replayed Houston's words over and over to himself. *"My friend..." He just called me his friend.*

"What is chute dogging?" Anne asked Benjamin on the drive home.

"No idea," he replied with a grin the size of Texas, "but I'm gonna find out."

Later, as Anne put the sandwich meat and trimmings out on the table for supper, Benjamin heard Anne ask her husband, Walter, if he would like to go with them over to Benjamin's new friend's house.

Halfway looking up from his computer, no doubt catching up on the daily events and trying to answer his wife at the same time, he replied, "Not tonight, honey."

Stopping what she was doing, Anne asked him what was so interesting in the computer news feed this evening. Putting the computer down, Walter looked up at Anne and told her, "It seems like our little community has become a thoroughfare for drugs being moved. The law enforcement agencies are stumped and cannot figure out how they are moving them. Think I'll call Sheriff Russell and see if I can get an update."

Anne replied, "Okay, suit yourself. After supper, Benjamin and I are off to Houston's house."

* * *

Turning onto Sherwood Drive, both Anne and Benjamin started watching the addresses on the mailboxes.

"Well, look at this," Anne exclaimed. "Houston lives where that tall tower-looking thing is." Pulling into the driveway and seeing a sea of pickups lined down it, she remarked, "He really does live close to us."

Following the driveway to the back of the house, right past the barn, Benjamin could see a cloud of dust. He figured this must be the arena.

Walking up to it, there were horses and what looked like cows with horns, lots of teenagers, and some parents. Benjamin stood there and watched for a few minutes, taking in the scene before him. Everyone, whether they were in the arena or not, was laughing and having fun. Something Benjamin hadn't done in a long time.

About that time, Houston looked up and saw Benjamin. He waved, hollering, "Hey, Benjamin, you made it! I'll be over there in a few minutes."

Benjamin returned the wave and nodded his head in agreement.

In a few minutes, just like he promised, Houston made his way over to where Benjamin and Anne were standing. "Mrs. Richards, you're more than welcome to sit in one of the lawn chairs if you want to, ma'am, and Benjamin can either climb over the fence or walk down to the gate and come in the arena." As he watched Benjamin back up, Benjamin could see that Houston realized his discomfort.

Speaking up quickly, Houston said, "We are taking a 15-minute break to let all the guys catch their breath and get a drink of water. So, you have perfect timing. This will give me a chance to introduce you to the rodeo team."

As Benjamin walked towards the arena gate, he watched two men on horses put all the cows with horns over in a side area, out of the arena. Not wanting to pass up a chance to make more friends, Benjamin decided he had better suck it up and do as Houston said. Houston met him at the gate and told him to come on in.

"Let me explain what all we are doing here," he said. "First, let me introduce you to the guys and my dad."

Walking towards the chute, Benjamin could see that everyone was standing around and having a drink of water, talking about their run.

"Hey, everybody, this is my friend Benjamin," Houston said. "Benjamin, this is everybody."

Benjamin spoke up after being introduced and said, "I sure hope there isn't a test. Don't know if I can remember all y'all's names."

The guys started laughing and assured him there would be no test. One of the guys was named Patrick, but Benjamin soon realized everyone referred to him as "Big P." He figured he got this nickname due to his size, as he was one big man.

Big P spoke up and said, "Benjamin, we are glad you are here. And as far as names go, you can call me Patrick, or you can call me Big P. Heck, you can call me anything you want, as long as it's not late for supper." Laughter broke out from everyone there. Big P, in Benjamin's estimation, was older than the other boys, yet younger than Houston's dad. His mind was full of questions to ask.

About that time, Houston's dad hollered, "Okay, boys, break is over. Back to practice."

Houston pointed for Benjamin to sit up on the top rail of the arena and watch. "After practice is over, you can ask me all the questions you want to, deal?"

Benjamin replied, "Deal."

For the rest of the evening, Benjamin watched all the guys, including Big P, take big ole cows and throw them to the ground. In his estimation, he thought it wouldn't be too much trouble for Big P, but some of the boys were even shorter than he was. Benjamin just couldn't figure out how they were doing it. That became the first question on his list to ask Houston.

An hour later, Big P hollered, "Okay, guys, this is the last pen of cattle for tonight! Once we are finished, let's get them fed, hayed, watered, and turned out until our next practice."

After the last cow was thrown to the ground, the group looked like a well-oiled machine going to work. Listening intently to the guys talking, Benjamin quickly learned that some of them were taking off what they called "wraps" from the cows' horns. Some were putting feed in the troughs, some were setting out a big round bale of hay, and a couple were dragging hoses up to fill the water trough. Everyone had a job to do, and it literally took no time at all when they pulled together like that.

After everyone left and all the dust settled, Houston and Big P were the only ones left in the arena. Houston asked Benjamin, "So what did you think? Want to give it a go?"

Benjamin looked at Houston and Big P. "I don't know…I'm kinda small, aren't I?"

Big P spoke up and said, "Son, if I can teach this little shrimp, Houston, I can teach you."

With eyes as big as saucers, Benjamin responded back, "Do you really think you can?"

Turning to walk towards his pickup, Big P hollered out, "You bet your bottom dollar I can!"

Benjamin was almost sad to see the night end. He actually had a scary—but good—time.

It seemed that Houston was feeling the same way. Speaking up, Houston asked Mrs. Richards if Benjamin could hang out for a while longer. His dad had apparently said he would be glad to bring Benjamin home later that night.

Anne looked at her foster son's face of hope, and she agreed.

Chapter 10

Benjamin

All the noise of the evening was gone. No one was talking, hollering, or laughing. Dust had settled down in the practice pen, and the cattle and horses were busy eating their feed and hay.

Houston's dogs were laying around. One in particular, Buddy, sat by Benjamin and continued rolling over to have his belly rubbed. You could see the lightning bugs against the backdrop of night as they floated over the pasture on the summer breeze. Benjamin thought that if peace had a fragrance or feeling, this was it—pure and simple.

"Hey, you're gonna spoil him if you keep rubbing his belly," Houston said.

Benjamin grinned. "He reminds me of my dog."

"What kind is your dog?" Houston asked.

"He's a German Shepherd, and he has become my best friend," Benjamin admitted. "My case worker suggested to my foster parents that it could help me adjust."

"What's your dog's name?" Houston asked.

"Well, the worker at the shelter asked me the same thing for their paperwork. After thinking about it for a few minutes, it came to me. I had no one, then the Richards picked me, and I became their foster kid. So, I figured this dog had no one and I picked him. That makes him a foster dog, right?"

"That makes sense to me," Houston said. "So what is his name?"

Benjamin said proudly, "I named him Foster!"

With a nod of his head, Houston said, "That's a great name. Oh, by the way, I realized I know Mr. Richards, your foster dad. That's where most all the rodeo kids get their hay. To be honest with you, until the other day after school, I had never met your foster mom. I was telling my parents about her, and that's when my mom realized—Mrs. Richards is the nice lady who works at the bank."

Benjamin felt it was only right to tell Houston his background, so he did. After listening intently to Benjamin's story for several minutes, Houston just sat there staring at him.

"Man, you have had a tough life, my friend," Houston said. "I am so sorry, but let me show you something." He pulled out his phone and showed Benjamin a post on social media that came across earlier that day.

"You can't go back and change the beginning, but you can start where you are and change the ending."

Tears began to well up in Benjamin's eyes, and as Benjamin turned to Houston, it was evident his new friend had sympathetic tears in his own eyes.

"Where did you find that?" Benjamin asked.

"It's a post from American Hat Company. I follow them," Houston said.

Looking at Houston's phone, and after wiping his eyes, Benjamin asked, "What's the American Hat Company? And what does that '+' and 'x' mark mean?"

"The short version is '+x'—positive times. It basically stands for this: it's a daily choice and reminder to renew yourself to begin again and put positive energy into the world. When we put these patches on our hats, well, it means we believe and live it. Don't believe me? Go look on their website, americanhat.net, and you can read all about it yourself."

Houston continued, "You need to follow them on social media. It's funny how everything they post always seems to have an impact on me."

Benjamin smiled back at Houston and said, "You're right, my friend. I will go follow them today."

Plopping down on a bale of hay, Houston asked, "Okay, everyone is gone, so tell me…What did you think? Did you like the guys and chute dogging?"

Benjamin replied, "To be honest, while I do have several questions, I am still putting all the pieces together. I've never been to a rodeo and really don't know much about it."

"Let me give you a quick tour of a rodeo, my friend," Houston began. "You have girls' events, and you have boys' events. Girls usually run barrels and poles, while some compete in team roping and ribbon roping. Then, there is goat tying, which is like calf roping that us boys do. Only boys can compete in calf roping, chute dogging, steer wrestling, and rough stock events."

"What's a rough stock event?" Benjamin asked.

"That's bareback or saddle bronc riding a horse. And then everyone's favorite…bull riding."

"Okay," Houston continued, "as Pastor Leo has often said, let 'er rip, tater chip! Give me your questions, and I will give you the answers."

"Well to start with, why do you put those wrap things on the cows?" Benjamin asked.

Laughing out loud, Houston said, "To start with, those are not cows; they are steers. And those 'wrap things' help protect the steers' heads when they are being roped. Usually, the same steers that are used for chute dogging are the same ones used for team roping."

Glancing from the dog and back over to Houston, Benjamin asked, "Do you team rope too?"

Houston smiled and said, "Well, let's say I try. I'm not very good at it, but I am learning. My friend, tell me what's really on your mind."

Benjamin paused for a long moment before asking, "Do you really think I could learn to chute dog, Houston?" He hoped Houston couldn't hear the despair in his voice.

Houston looked at his friend. "Well, let me tell you about Big P. His real name is Patrick. However, we have three Patricks associated with this team. Like I said, we have Big Patrick, then we have 'MP' and 'LP.'"

Benjamin started laughing and said, "Let me guess…Middle Patrick and Little Patrick?"

"You got it!" Houston laughed back. "Anyway, Big P, back in his day, was on this same rodeo team for all four of his high school years. You can tell by his sheer size that he could throw any steer to the ground; however, he will tell you it's all about technique. Size really doesn't play that big of a part in chute dogging. You and I are about the same size, and just like Big P said, if he could teach me, he can teach you. Want to give it a try?"

It only took Benjamin a few seconds to nod his head yes in response.

"Okay, don't forget to mark your calendars for our practice nights, and don't worry—I can work with you any night or day of the week," Houston said. Benjamin just smiled.

"First things first," he continued. "I want to introduce you to the rest of the rodeo team. You met many of them here tonight, but there are more. We have an end-of-year awards banquet, get-togethers for cookouts, children's hospital visits to play games with the kids, and we do volunteer work in our community and r-o-d-e-o! Come to think of it, it's just like Miss Donna teaches us. We are a rodeo family not only during our high school years, but we also build friendships that last a lifetime.

"Okay, Benjamin, since you are going to be on the rodeo team, we have to make sure you are properly dressed in 'rodeo dress code,' which means a trip to the local Western store and The Best Hat Store, which carries the American Hat."

Benjamin asked, "Why the American Hat?"

"Because that's what this rodeo family wears, and you, my friend, are a part of our rodeo family—now and forever more. Hey, how about Saturday, Benjamin? We could go then."

"Probably…As long as my chores are done, my foster mom will say yes," Benjamin said.

Looking over at Benjamin, Houston asked, "Oh, by the way, wanta go to church with me on Sunday?"

"Sorry, my friend," Benjamin said. "My foster parents told me they have decided we are going to the church that sits on the north side of town. I think it's a Baptist church."

"Cool," Houston responded. "That's where my family goes, too, so I guess I will see you there!"

* * *

Sure enough, as Benjamin and his foster parents walked into the church on Sunday, there was Houston and his family. Walking over and greeting Benjamin, Houston hollered out, "Long time, no see!"

Laughing out loud, Benjamin replied back, "Not since yesterday!"

"Dude, you look pretty sharp in your jeans, button-down shirt, and American Hat."

"I have to admit it feels good, but I'm not used to wearing a hat," Benjamin answered.

"Don't worry, you will get used to it," Houston said. "Trust me, you will get to a point where you feel naked without it."

"Guess I better go sit down," Benjamin said. "Looks like church is about to start."

"Wait a minute; just wait a minute!" Houston responded. "The rodeo team sits over there." He pointed to a couple of pews over to the side of the auditorium.

Benjamin turned to his foster mom to ask for permission, and she nodded her head yes. Smiling at her, Benjamin turned and followed Houston over to where the rodeo team was sitting.

As they waited for church to begin, Houston pointed out all the members of the church, giving Benjamin the lowdown on each one.

"There's a special group of ladies I call the Prayer Chain. I want to introduce you to them, but that will have to wait until after church."

"After church?" Benjamin repeated.

Houston said, "Oh, yes! Today the church is having a social, which means we get to eat a lot of great food. When the Prayer Chain is in charge, you can bet your bottom dollar it will be the best food you have ever eaten. Trust me!"

* * *

Pastor Leo closed out the service with a prayer over the social's food so that everyone could go straight into the fellowship hall, get their plate of food, and chow down.

Standing in line, Benjamin couldn't wait any longer, so he asked Houston, "Why do you call them the Prayer Chain?"

Houston said, "Here in a few minutes, you will see. Other than the fact that they get together and pray every week, let me show you something else."

Picking up their plates and eating utensils, they took their place in the buffet line. The first lady serving the food was apparently Miss Shelly Belle, who Houston introduced as a retired English literature professor and member of the Prayer Chain. Benjamin stepped in front of her to get his serving of mashed potatoes with cream gravy.

"Young man," Miss Shelly Belle began, "it is my sincere hope and desire that you have visited the sanitary facilities and, under temperatures of at least 90 degrees, scrubbed each digit profusely for a minimum of at least 60 seconds to ensure all germs and bacteria have been dealt with properly."

Benjamin was shocked. All he could do was stand there and smile, not knowing what else to do. Looking back at Houston, he asked, "What did she just say?"

Another woman, who Benjamin would later come to know as Miss Clara Mae, put a helping of corn on his plate. She said, "She was asking if you had washed your hands."

As each lady put a helping of food on their plates, Houston would say, "Thank you, Miss Edith Louise; thank you, Miss Betty Sue; thank you, Miss Judy Kay; thank you, Miss Patricia Ann; thank you, Miss Ruby May; thank you, Miss Clara Mae," and as they approached the last lady, Houston said, "Thank you, Miss Bev."

With a perplexed look, Benjamin asked Houston, "Miss Bev... Where is her second name like all the other ladies?"

Miss Bev must have overheard and interjected, "Sweetie, I may have not been born in Texas, but I got here as fast as I could!" As if on cue, the entire Prayer Chain started giggling. "On a serious note, we did move here when I was little girl. I remember asking my daddy why I didn't have a 'second name,' and he told me it was because I was born in the winter, and it froze off!" Once again, all the Prayer Chain ladies broke into giggles.

Not really thinking Miss Bev was all that funny, the boys decided it would be in their best interest to join in and laugh with them. Benjamin didn't want the ladies to be upset with him when it came time to dish out the dessert.

As the two boys went to sit down at a table, Benjamin asked, "How do you remember all those names?"

"Well to be honest," Houston responded, "it took me a long time to remember all their names. It was kinda funny. In the beginning, one time when I couldn't remember their names, I referred to them as 'the blue-haired ladies.' They let me know immediately they didn't like that, so we made an agreement. I wouldn't call them the blue-haired ladies, and they wouldn't call me a kid. Our arrangement has worked out well. Now that I think about it, I believe they really like being called the Prayer Chain Ladies." Leaning across the table and almost whispering, Houston quietly let Benjamin know that the word around the community was, don't mess with the Prayer Chain. These ladies were evidently very special and not to be messed with.

"Come to think of it," Houston went on between bites of food, "it's like the Prayer Chain always knows when to show up. I asked my mom, and she said it's that 'woman intuition thing.'"

"Oh," Benjamin responded. "That makes sense."

Just then, Miss Donna walked by the table with her plate of food. She told Benjamin how nice he looked and not to forget the rodeo meeting tomorrow night. Looking up at Miss Donna, both boys responded, "Yes, ma'am," at the same time.

"Oh man, I almost forgot," Houston said. "Benjamin, we've got to take care of your ticket."

Benjamin's eyes grew wide. "A ticket? I can't even drive yet!"

Laughing loudly, Houston responded, "A ticket is an amateur radio license."

"A what?" Benjamin asked.

"We'll fill you in later, but trust me, you're gonna love it!"

Chapter 11

Benjamin

Benjamin had never hung out around a campfire, much less had an amateur radio license. Come to think of it, he had never really done much of anything like other kids his age. But since being placed with the Richards and meeting the rodeo team, his whole world had changed. As the fire reflected in his eyes, Benjamin reflected on his first invitation to hang out with the rodeo team down at the "No Gotty."

Getting in the pickup, Benjamin felt like he knew Houston well enough to ask why the arena was called the "No Gotty."

With his arm resting on the steering wheel as he shifted gears, a smile came across Houston's face as if lost in a memory.

"Well, Benjamin," he began, "back in the day, there was no water, no bathroom, no electricity. Us guys were okay with it, but the girls... Well, let's just say that was a different story. So, the arena became known as the no gotty water, no gotty bathrooms, and no gotty electricity. Even after Miss Donna got all the modern conveniences of life installed at her arena, well, we couldn't bring ourselves to change the name. Kinda like an old pair of boots, it was already broken in, comfortable. And when it rains, we just hold our meeting in the barn. Sometimes we all show up just to hang out together. Miss Donna said she didn't mind at all."

Benjamin came out of his trance when he heard the rest of the team members walk up. He quickly realized he felt relaxed around everyone. Could this mean he was really becoming a part of this rodeo family, like Houston had said?

As the team approached the fire pit, Brady looked at Benjamin and asked, "Did you get your call sign?"

Bending at the waist as if to bow, Benjamin said in a very formal voice, "You may now call me Q5VLN." As he straightened up, the whole team started applauding. Benjamin felt a surge of pride.

All the guys were laughing and started talking about school, rodeo, girls, and all that had been going on in their lives when the subject came around to parents. Brady talked about how strict his parents were. According to him, his parents watched him like a hawk, constantly asking, "Did you do your homework? Did you make your bed? Did you brush your teeth? Did you feed the dogs?"

Poking the fire with a small stick that had been laying on the ground beside him, Tyler said, "Man, do I hear you. That's all I hear from my parents, too. What's up with all the orders?"

Houston interjected, "Hey, guys, maybe we're looking at this all wrong. I used to think the same thing about my parents, but if you stop and think, is it all mean? Maybe they are looking out for us, you know, for our future."

Swinging his head around as if on a swivel, Bubba barked back, "Have you lost your mind? Yes, sir, I think you have lost your ever-loving mind!" The consensus around the campfire was one of agreement.

"Take the other night as an example," Houston said. "I pulled off the main road going down the driveway, and just like clockwork, all the exterior lights were on—the solar ones my dad installed that line the driveway, the light on the front of the barn, and the back porch lights. Why, may you ask? Well, it's because my parents knew I would be coming in late from the rodeo and they made sure I wasn't coming home to a dark house. And when I walked in the back door, there on the kitchen table by a piece of paper with hearts on it was some milk and my favorite cookies my mom made for me. You know, guys, one of these days we are going to have to fend for ourselves. No one will be around to make sure we take care of all the little details of life. Trust me, it's the little things in life that mean so much."

Under his breath, Benjamin whispered, "I would give anything to have a family like he does."

Evidently, Houston was on a roll and decided he had more to say. "My parents have supported me and my big sister, Katy, in every sport and activity I can think of. There was T-ball, baseball, ballet, rodeo, gymnastics, guitar lessons, football." Looking up and across the campfire to see where the giggles were coming from, Houston could see a couple of the guys elbowing each other and trying to hold their laughter back.

Houston asked what was so funny, to which Bubba replied, "Can't seem to get the image of you in a pink leotard and tutu out of my mind!" The laughter was contagious, and everyone started laughing, even Houston.

One by one, each of the boys began describing their "parent war stories" to the group. When it was obvious that it was Benjamin's turn, Houston seemed to be able to read his friend's face. He knew he was dreading when it came his turn to share. Houston had heard Benjamin's story, after all, and he knew it wasn't good.

Coming to Benjamin's rescue, Houston spoke up, "Hey, guys, we need to put this fire out and get home. It's getting late. And I don't think any of us want to be grounded for breaking curfew, do we? But before we head out, I am asking all of you to keep my dad in your prayers, please. This whole drug trafficking thing has really been weighing heavy on him."

Brady asked if there was anything they could do to help, to which Houston replied, "I'm not sure. The best thing we can do is keep our eyes and ears open. Any leads would help him out. Thanks, everybody, I appreciate it."

Brady turned to Houston and said, “Let me remind you, my friend, that we are a rodeo team and ham radio operators. We look out for each other. This is no different. From this night forward, we pay attention to every little thing that looks out of the ordinary.”

Everyone began gathering up all the lawn chairs and putting them back in the barn for next week when Maddy said, “We need to think of something else fun to do. Take tonight as an example; the arena was too muddy from the rain last night, so we just sat around talking.”

While everyone brainstormed, Greg jumped off the tree stump he was sitting on, declaring, “I have an idea! I have some parts at my house that I can assemble to do an experiment that will tell us just how far you can talk to or follow an amateur radio set-up.”

In a flurry of excitement, he continued, “It’s called APRS, which stands for Automatic Packet Reporting System. That means I can put a radio in or on something that moves and track it on my computer.”

The consensus was that would be boring, as none of them ever leave town.

After thinking about it for a few minutes, Greg said, “Why don’t I put together a small radio equipped with APRS, a battery with a solar panel to keep it charged along with a magnetic antenna? We could put it on the bull wagon and see where all it goes.”

Bubba spoke up to ask, “Under the bull wagon?”

“No, not under it, on top,” Greg said. “That way, no one will know what we are doing. Besides, wouldn’t it be fun to see where the bull wagon travels going from rodeo to rodeo?”

“Sounds like a good plan,” Houston remarked. “We can put our experiment in motion at the rodeo this weekend. Does that give you enough time to build this contraption?”

Greg replied, “That gives me more than enough time. Now we just have to figure out a way to get it on top of the bull wagon without getting caught. My parents would kill me!”

Bubba asked, “Do we want to put push pins on a map that shows everywhere the bull wagon travels?”

Houston replied back, "Not on my bedroom wall. Don't want my mother yelling at me!"

"With this system," Greg replied, "I can print the map off, showing every location the bull wagon travels, and we can put it on the board here at the No Gotty."

"What is an APRS?" Ariel asked.

Chuckling, Greg replied, "It's a small transceiver that will send out a beacon on frequency 144.390 MHZ on a regular programmed interval… like every minute or five minutes, anything we want. In the data stream, it will give the GPS location, altitude, and speed of whatever it's attached to, along with the call sign of the owner of the unit, which would be me, Q5AGN. We can follow it once the APRS data starts coming in on my computer."

Maddy broke in, "This will be fun for us since we don't ever get to leave town! Kinda an adventure, like Mr. Rex talked about. We get to go on a trip and never leave home!"

As Houston put out the last ember of fire, Greg asked if everyone agreed, to which everyone said yes.

"First, we need to decide who is climbing on top of the trailer," Bubba said. "I guess it goes without saying, it has to be Greg…and who else?"

Benjamin spoke up and said, "I volunteer."

Maddy said, "I can stand watch to let you know if anyone is coming."

The rest of the team would walk by in intervals, talking and thereby creating a distraction to help cover up any noise Greg and Benjamin might make putting the transceiver in place.

When Madison raised her hand, everyone knew to get really quiet, or else they wouldn't be able to hear her. "What do y'all want me to do?" she asked.

Maddy looked at Madison and said, "Aren't you the wrangler in goat tying this weekend?"

Madison nodded her head yes.

"Good," Maddy said. "Go get the goats out of their trailer a little earlier than what you would usually do. Walk them right by the bull wagon and stand there a while. Act like you are having to wait to take them to the arena. All the bleating they do will help cover up any noise the guys make on top of the trailer."

The rest of the team agreed. Next rodeo weekend, they would put their plan into action! With that, everyone said goodnight and left the No Gotty.

* * *

Pulling up in front of Benjamin's house, Houston said, "Here you go, my friend. Guess I will see you tomorrow."

"Hey, thanks for the ride, Houston," Benjamin said. "And also, thank you for stepping in. I didn't particularly want to tell my story to everyone just yet."

"No worries, my friend, no worries," Houston replied. "Oh, by the way, I have entered you in chute dogging at the next rodeo."

Standing there like a frozen statue, Benjamin was horrified and at a loss for words. Before he could say anything, Houston hollered through the truck window, "Look here, Benjamin! You have been practicing; it's time to get your feet wet. You got this, my friend. I believe in you."

Benjamin stood there trying to hold back his tears. No one had ever told him they believed in him; no one. Miss Donna's words were starting to make sense to him, about this being a rodeo *family*. And now, it was a ham radio family.

Chapter 12

Benjamin

"Well, today's the day, Benjamin. You are up tonight in chute dogging!" exclaimed Houston. "Now don't you worry; we will all be right there helping you out."

"Are you sure about this?" Benjamin asked in a strained voice.

Putting his hand on Benjamin's shoulder, Houston answered him back, "Look at me. Look at me in the eyes. When you come out of that chute, take all your hostility and channel it. Remember everything Big P taught us, and stay focused."

Walking from the concession stand area over to the north end of the arena, something caught Benjamin's eye, so much so that it stopped him in his tracks. Scanning the crowd and looking at every man there, he thought to himself, *Was that Uncle Bruce? Sure looked like that crazy hat he always wore. Nah, it couldn't be, could it? My eyes must be playing tricks on me.*

Listening to everyone holler his name snapped Benjamin back to reality as he tried to focus on the next few seconds of his life. He walked through the gate into the arena and over to the roping chutes. Benjamin could hear people in all directions calling his name.

There sat his foster parents, Richard and Anne. They, too, were screaming and shouting his name. They were cheering him on. All his rodeo teammates were out there with him too, each cheering him on in their own special way.

Just as Benjamin thought to himself, *I cannot let my rodeo family down*, the announcer said his name. Assuming the position, the last thing he heard was Big P saying, "Channel everything and use it!"

Benjamin nodded his head, calling for his steer, and out of the chute they shot. All his teammates were shouting and cheering; he could hear every one of them. Out of nowhere, a strength came over him that he could not put into words. And then, BAM! Down that steer went, smack dab on its side with all four feet facing the same direction.

Benjamin got up and looked back towards the dogging chute. He could see all his teammates jumping up and down. He looked over in the stands, and there were his foster parents doing the same thing! What a wonderful feeling, a feeling he had never experienced before in his whole life. A feeling he never wanted to lose.

Running back to the chute, he jumped up in the air, hollering, "I did it! I did it!" Looking up at Big P, he said, "Thank you, sir."

Slapping him on the back, Big P replied, "Son, we are a rodeo family, and this is what we do. We work with and cheer everyone on, whether it's a good run or maybe not so good of a run. You tried your best to do everything I taught you, maybe a few bobbles here and there. Bottom line is, I am proud of you. Can't wait until next week. Maybe you can shave some more time off your run. We will work on that in the practice pen at the No Gotty."

With a sense of pride, Benjamin responded, "Yes, sir, you bet we will."

Houston ran up to Benjamin next. "Dude, awesome job!" he said. "Where in the world did that come from? One second that steer had your dirt surfing, and the next you laid him out."

"Guess I did what I was told to do," Benjamin said. "Channel everything, and trust me, I had a lot to channel. I'll be right back! I'm going over to the horse trailer to get Foster out and let him walk around."

Giving Benjamin a thumbs up, Houston headed on over to the concession stand to get something to eat.

Walking up to the horse trailer, Benjamin saw Foster wagging his tail so hard and fast, he had to tell him to slow down before his tail flew off. Benjamin put the leash on his best furry friend, then they started heading back over to the arena to watch the rest of the rodeo.

Just like before, the closer they got to the bull wagon, Foster started pulling on the leash almost to the point of dragging Benjamin with him. Holding him with both hands, it was taking every ounce of strength Benjamin had in his body to control Foster. He could not figure out why Foster did this; it was only by the bull wagons that he acted this way.

Benjamin felt kind of embarrassed when everyone started staring at him. It looked like his dog was going crazy. "Note to self," he spoke out loud, "stop going by the bull wagons!"

* * *

Donna

With chute dogging now over with, barrel racing was next. There was a first timer in this event, too: Ariel. Making her way down to the south end of the arena, Donna thought to herself, *Hmm, the stock contractor must have hired new people to drive the bull wagons and other rough stock trailers.* She didn't think these were the same drivers as last rodeo season.

Making her way to the back holding pen of the arena, Donna quickly found Ariel. You could spot her anywhere, with her beautiful, long, dirty blonde hair braided down her back, almost reaching the cantle on the back of the saddle, riding a gorgeous yellow horse—which to anyone outside of the rodeo world would be called a palomino—and the look of fear was all over Ariel's face.

Donna knew only too well what getting ready to make your very first rodeo run could do to a person. Hopefully Ariel's run would go well like Benjamin's.

For a split second, Donna's mind wandered back to the first time she backed into the Heeler's box at a roping, which helped her understand everything that was going through Ariel's body and mind. Her horse knew what was coming up, and his blood was pumping hard. The only thing on Donna's mind in this moment was to try and help Ariel and her horse stay calm.

In somewhat of a squeaky voice and with tears welling up in her blue-gray eyes, Ariel said, "Miss Donna, I don't think I can do this. As a matter of fact, I think I'm gonna throw up! I can't do this, I can't do this!"

Over the speakers, Donna could hear the rodeo announcer calling out the run order of the girls running barrels that night. He said, "Ariel, you are on deck," meaning she was the next competitor.

Donna led her and her horse up to the alley. "Can't never could do anything, and if you're gonna throw up, do it on the other side of your horse and not on me!" she said. "Your horse feels and smells fear."

It appeared Ariel had been shocked out of her head and back into reality.

"Ariel," Donna said in a softer voice, "trust in your horse, and trust in yourself. You have been preparing for today for a long time. See the run in front of you, sweetie. You can do this. I have faith in you."

After hearing the announcer call her name, Ariel looked at Donna as if she had something to say, but no words would come out. Seeing the hesitation in her eyes, Donna turned loose of the reins and stepped back, hollering, "Ride like you stole him!"

That's all it took. With her facial expression having changed from scared to determined and her blue eyes having turned to solid gray, Ariel shot down that alleyway, exploding into the arena with a run that was textbook perfect. First barrel clean, second barrel clean, third barrel clean...

Everyone hollered as she came off her third barrel, "Kick, bring him home, kick!"

Everyone was clearing the alleyway for Ariel to exit the arena. She stopped her horse before she hit the back gate. Once she got her horse in check and calmed down, the back gate opened and let her out.

In the warm-up area in the back, Donna waited for Ariel with a big smile, beaming with pride at not only Ariel's accomplishment, but more importantly, overcoming her fears. She had done it—broken through her fear and proved to herself that nothing was impossible. She just had to believe in herself.

Walking out of the warm-up pen, Donna saw what looked like flashlights by one of the bull wagons that was backed up to the loading dock. Just as she was about to go investigate these unusual lights, she heard her name being called out: "Donna! Hey, Donna, over here."

Turning her attention from the lights, Donna saw Ariel's parents walk toward her. It was easy to see, even in just the glow of the arena lights, how excited they were. They were yelling, "*She did it, she did it!*"

Seeing their admiration for their daughter was worth all the work that had led up to that night, Donna thought. Those mysterious lights over by the bull pen had moved to the back of her mind.

Chapter 13

Houston

Pulling off the main road onto the long, winding driveway leading down to the house and barn, Houston noticed that all the usual lights had been left on, which brought a smile to his face. He even laughed out loud a little bit.

Repeatedly he told his parents they didn't have to do that, to which their response was always, "We do it because we love you, son."

His mother had said, "You may not understand the 'why we do it' now, but give it a few years and you will." As she turned to look at Houston's dad, they both said in unison, "Trust me; you will."

Late-night rodeo was now a part of Houston's life, and it brought him comfort knowing the lights would be on when he came home. This was one of the many small ways his parents showed him how much they cared about him.

He loved the fact that while his mother was always there to watch him compete and cheer him on, whenever his dad made it out to the arena, it set his adrenaline to overload as he was competing not only for himself but also in some small way for them, too. Both of Houston's parents had stood beside him and his sister in all their various endeavors. With Katy away at college, he now had their full and undivided attention.

After putting the pickup in park and turning the engine off, Houston sat there for a few moments, glad to be home but mostly glad he had a place to come home to.

Walking across the yard, stopping only to pet his dogs, Houston was anxious to shower and get on to bed; it had been a very long day, beginning with school, some exams, and then competing at rodeo.

As Houston made sure the back door was locked, he could see the light from the desk lamp escaping from under the door of his dad's office. Recognizing the source of the light, he realized his dad's late-night hours had become more frequent, which in his mind meant there was something going on. It seemed that being the Sheriff was a much heavier burden than Houston first understood; it was all on his dad's shoulders. Something more than lost dogs and writing speeding tickets had to be going on.

Sticking his head in the door confirmed his suspicion that his dad was working late again. There he sat with furrowed brows and a frown on his face. This told Houston something was weighing on his mind right now.

In somewhat of a whisper, Houston softly spoke up, "Dad, are you busy?"

Looking up from his desk, his dad's frown was quickly replaced with a smile upon seeing Houston standing there. "Come on in, son."

As Houston entered the room and took the seat by his dad's desk, he asked, "Dad, is there anything I can do to help?"

Smiling at Houston, he replied, "Son, that means a lot to me, but to be honest, I don't know if anyone can help right now."

"At least let me try," was Houston response.

Glancing at the papers scattered all over his desk, Houston's dad looked back at him. "Well, it seems someone is using our town to transport fentanyl. Every lead we get takes us to a one-way street to a dead end. It's like these people are either ghosts flying overhead, digging tunnels underground, or ordinary people driving right in front of our eyes. And to be honest, son, it's frustrating. After all these years in law enforcement, I am beginning to think there is finally a crime that may have me beat."

With a look of shock on his face, Houston sat there in silence. He had never seen his dad like this before.

"Sorry, son. I didn't mean to put all that on you."

"No, Dad, you don't have to be sorry," Houston replied. "Thank you for being honest with me. And I do have a piece of advice; that is, if you want my input."

Sheriff Russell's expression grew perplexed as he asked, "What would your advice be?" As he watched his son, he could see his facial expression change to a familiar one.

Houston said, "Dad, I'm gonna tell you what you tell me all the time. Go back to the beginning and start with what you know, paying close attention to details."

Rearing back in his chair and laughing out loud, Houston's dad replied, "Out of the mouths of babes! You know what, son, you are correct. Thanks for the reminder. Deputy Weldon should be back from his vacation soon, and with this becoming an all-hands-on-deck situation, he can't get back here soon enough."

He added, "Maybe a good night's sleep would help," and Houston said goodnight and left the room.

* * *

Sheriff Russell

Bright and early the next morning, Sheriff Russell was at his office, attempting to get a head start on the day. Trying to take his son's advice to heart, he went back to the beginning and started laying out all the information he had previously gathered.

Breaking his train of thought was Deputy Weldon strolling into his office. Sheriff Russell put a lot of faith in his officers and staff, especially Deputy Weldon.

As the Deputy took off his hat, the Sheriff realized they were neck in neck in the race of receding hairlines. He noticed the big grin on his Deputy's face and thought something was different. Leaning back in his office chair, he asked him, "What's going on? You look like the cat that ate the canary with that smile on your face."

With the biggest grin a man could have, Deputy Weldon blurted out, "I got married!"

Trying to keep from tipping over in his chair, Sheriff Russell hollered out, "What!? You got married? Weldon, you only went on vacation!"

Evidently not letting the negativity of his boss take away his wedded bliss, Deputy Weldon responded, "Crazy, isn't it, sir? It was love at first sight. Can you believe it, Sheriff? Two people from the same small town, and we ran into each other at that all-inclusive resort I went to!"

"From the same small town?" the Sheriff asked. "Who did you marry?"

As if he hadn't heard the question, Weldon went on to say, "Natalie had just bought the old Roberts' Ranch at the edge of town, and that's where we live now. My new little bride has completely remodeled, torn down, and added to that old place...and it looks great!"

The Sheriff just sat there for a few moments with many thoughts running through his head. His good friend was very tall, probably somewhere around six-foot-two, if he was to guess. He was a plain and simple man. Why, even the Prayer Chain ladies thought he would be a professional bachelor his whole life.

Breaking through the Sheriff's runaway thoughts, Deputy Weldon spoke up, "Look at the wedding gift she got me. It's a real gold Rolex watch. And before I forget, here's your invitation personally delivered for our housewarming party. Don't bring a gift! Trust me, we don't need it. Just want everyone to meet my new wife."

Taking the invitation from his hand, Sheriff Russell could only muster, "Congratulations, my friend, I am happy for you. I would not miss this party for anything in the world. Consider it marked on my calendar."

Deputy Weldon breathed a sigh of relief. "Okay, boss, how many speeding tickets in the school zone have been written in my absence, and how many times did someone have to go get Mrs. Wilson's cat down out of the tree in her front yard?"

"Deputy," the Sheriff replied, "we have a much bigger problem on our hands."

With a shocked look on his face, Deputy Weldon sat down and asked the Sheriff to bring him up to speed. Sheriff Russell laid out everything they had been sent from the FBI. "The bottom line is this, Deputy Weldon: whomever is transporting the drugs has decided their best route is right through our county. The question is, how? In a car, a truck, transport trucks? We can't stop every single vehicle on the highway to inspect it. It's like finding a needle in a haystack! If we could just get a break, anything..."

Deputy Weldon no doubt recognized the Sheriff's tone and body language, which meant long days and weekends of work until these drugs were off the street, and the criminals were behind bars. "I don't know how I'm going to explain all these long nights to my bride, but duty calls," he said.

Over the next few weeks, Sheriff Russell and Deputy Weldon followed every lead that came in on the tip line—but still nothing. Every evening before leaving the station, everyone would try to give encouragement and boost morale by saying, "We'll get 'em tomorrow."

* * *

Houston

It was clear that Houston's father was completely focused on these drug traffickers and not so much on his day-to-day routine.

As Houston headed out the door to school, his mom asked if he'd drop off his dad's lunch at the station, because he had forgotten it again.

Houston was happy to do so. As he walked into the outer office of the police station, he heard a familiar voice call out his name: "Houston, my boy, how have you been?"

Recognizing the voice of Sheriff Murphree, he turned to greet him. "I am good, sir. How are you doing today?"

"Well, son," Murphree responded as he headed towards the door, "I am good. As a matter of fact, if it gets any better, someone may write me a ticket!" Everyone in the receptionist area laughed.

"What brings you to our neck of the woods?" Houston asked.

Sheriff Murphree responded, "Well, let's just say we have some county line overlapping business… Back to work for me now!" And with that, he laughed and headed out the door.

Houston thought, *That man always has the best disposition of anyone I have ever met in my life.*

Walking into his dad's office, Houston saw that he was on the phone. He knew to be quiet and wait. Plopping himself down into a chair, he began surveying the room, smiling at the various awards his dad had been given throughout the years, as well as pictures of their family. Then, Houston's attention was drawn to a big map on the wall.

The map had a bunch of push pins in it, and Houston remembered Mr. Rex's story about the map on the wall at his home. Then, something caught his eye because it looked like something he had seen before. About this time, his dad was getting off the phone, but a light bulb had lit up in Houston's mind. The push pins marked the different locations where all the rodeos were held.

Sheriff Russell thanked his son for dropping off his lunch, then asked him what was so interesting about the map that drew his intensive attention.

Houston responded, "Wow, Dad, it's all the cities across the state where the rodeos are being held. I didn't realize you kept up with all my rodeo stuff! I guess you're getting ready for when I hit the pro circuit. Well, I gotta get to school! See ya tonight!"

Houston smiled and headed out the door. He could not know that his words had sparked a light bulb in his father's mind, too—that all the pieces had just fit into place for the Sheriff.

And he did not hear his father's quietly spoken words: "Thank you, son."

Chapter 14

Benjamin

Walking into the house after school, Benjamin set about taking care of his chores. Then it would be on to homework, hopefully finishing in time for supper.

As the family sat down at the table and prayed over the food, the conversation quickly went from, "How was your day at school or work?" to "Have y'all seen the new Mrs. Weldon?" Both Benjamin and his foster dad shook their heads no, so Anne apparently decided to fill them in.

"Well, let me tell you about her," she began. "She is absolutely beautiful! Gorgeous long, black hair, hourglass figure, meticulously painted fingernails, and her clothes–oh, don't get me started on her clothes!

"The first time I saw her, I thought she was a runway model. She didn't walk into the bank lobby; she floated in. I tell you, I bet she was a model at some time in her life. And while I am not allowed to give out any specific information on her, I can tell you this: she is filthy rich. I look forward to her coming in every Monday morning, not only to make her 'large' deposits, but all of us ladies at the bank cannot wait to see what she will wear next. Why, I would go so far as to bet she has not worn the same outfit twice!

"When we all realized who she was married to, well, let's just say it had to be love, because it wasn't based on Deputy Weldon's good looks, that's for sure. I can't wait for the housewarming party she is throwing. She invited everyone at the bank! And I am told the 'who's who' of the county—from the Judge, the Mayor, to the Commissioner's Court—will be there. Her home will probably look like something out of one of those fancy magazines. Why, I may get some decorating ideas for our home."

* * *

"Yes, siree, your foster mom was right," Houston said to Benjamin. "All the 'who's who' of town must be here."

Anne and the two boys walked through the sea of cars lining the street and massive driveway of the Weldons' new home.

Laughing out loud, Benjamin replied, "Guess they want all of us to see how rich they are."

"Benjamin, let's not talk like that, son. It's rude," Anne whispered.

He replied, "Yes, ma'am. Sorry."

As the three of them approached the beveled glass with beautifully wrought, iron-trimmed front doors, a man all dressed up in a black butler's uniform opened the door, welcoming them in before they could even press the doorbell.

Leaning between the boys so both of them could hear her, Anne whispered, "Boys, don't touch anything in this house, do you understand me?"

Benjamin and Houston just nodded their heads yes in awe as words escaped them. They continued to look around the room. Benjamin thought, *And this is just the entry foyer!*

* * *

Sheriff Russell

After the tour of the newlyweds' home was given to everyone, Sheriff Russell asked his Deputy if they could have a private conversation.

The two men walked into what Sheriff Russell assumed was a library. Deputy Weldon invited his boss to take a seat.

"Deputy, I am hoping you don't get upset with me, but I must ask you a question," Sheriff Russell said carefully.

"Okay, ask away," was Weldon's response.

Taking a deep breath, the Sheriff asked, "How are you able to live this lavish lifestyle on a deputy's salary?"

"Oh, Sheriff, is that all you wanted to know?" Weldon laughed. "Sir, it's all my wife's money; her family is loaded. As a matter of fact, I asked her the same question, and that's when she told me in confidence that she is from old money, from back East. To be honest, sir, I can't touch any of her money. Heck, I'm not on any of her checking accounts. As a matter of fact, I still have my original checking account from when I started working at the Sheriff's Department years ago. Bottom line is—while our sheets mingle in the washing machine, our money doesn't."

"Oh," Sheriff Russell said. "I see."

And with that, Deputy Weldon said that they had better get back to the party. Nodding his head in agreement, Sheriff Russell followed him out of the library.

* * *

Maddy, Ariel, and Madison

The afternoon at the Weldon residence was like something out of a movie: important people standing around talking politics, businesspeople talking about the stock market, church leaders discussing theology and upcoming meetings, school events, and various other people they had never seen before who were obviously very wealthy by the way they dressed and acted. Ladies of the town, specifically the Prayer Chain ladies, scrutinized every piece of furniture and decor in the mansion to see if it was indeed "the real thing" or a "knock off." Waiters walked around with trays of little sandwiches, desserts, and drinks.

Needing to use the "little girls' room," Maddy and Ariel walked up behind the new Mrs. Weldon, tapping her on the shoulder to ask where it was located. As the lady turned around, Maddy quickly realized it wasn't Mrs. Weldon.

"I'm sorry!" Maddy said. "I thought you were Mrs. Weldon."

With somewhat of a huffy attitude, the lady responded, "I am not Mrs. Weldon. I am Mrs. Moore, the head of staff for Mrs. Weldon. What do you children need?"

"Just looking for the little girls' room, ma'am," Maddy said.

Pointing with long, painted fingernails, Mrs. Moore told them, "Down the hall, second door on the right."

With a quick "thank you, ma'am," Maddy and Ariel got away from her as quickly as possible. Making their way down the long hallway, Ariel looked over at Maddy and said, "I could have sworn that was the new Mrs. Weldon, couldn't you?"

"Yes, definitely!" was Maddy's response. "From the back, they literally look the same, don't they?"

Over in one corner of the main room, the rodeo team moms were talking. They all laughed out loud when one of the moms asked, "Are we supposed to hold our pinky out when we drink our punch?"

Just on the other side of the doorway stood Madison, listening intently.

Not knowing that anyone was close enough to hear what was intended to be a private gossip session, Rachel, a bank teller in town, addressed some of the other ladies who also worked at the bank, saying, "All that money in the bank, this beautiful mansion along with the meticulous grounds and horse barns, two highly polished black SUVs in the garage, a housekeeper, servants, an arena and gardens…Mrs. Weldon must be from old, old money, and a lot of it."

Anne, Benjamin's foster mom, pointed out in a somewhat hushed tone, "Let's not forget all those cash deposits she brings in every Monday morning like clockwork."

Rachel interrupted Anne, "Don't forget—her head housekeeper makes weekly deposits as well."

“True,” Anne responded. “That’s true, but I have a question. Having old family money is one thing, but what’s up with all the cash deposits on a weekly basis? Where is all that money coming from?”

“Interesting, to say the least,” another woman responded, and all the other ladies agreed.

Madison knew she had to tell the rest of the rodeo team what she had just heard.

The Prayer Chain appeared to be having their own conversation about the day’s events. Madison walked by them as they were seated in the formal living room.

“Almost didn’t realize the head housekeeper was indeed a housekeeper,” one lady was saying. “She’s dressed to the nines. Don’t know how she does all the housework with those long nails and fancy shoes.”

A lady who Madison recognized as Miss Thelma Louise commented, “Well, let’s not forget she has a whole staff of people to give orders to.”

“Well, being the head housekeeper must pay really well,” Miss Patricia Ann said, to which everyone giggled.

Miss Bev’s observation was, “I think we are all in the wrong business!”

Setting her teacup down on the saucer, Miss Patricia Ann interjected, “Ladies, I taught Deputy Weldon in high school, and I can assure you he had no chance of getting a girlfriend back then, much less this beautiful wife.”

Miss Shelly Belle said, “It surpasses all understanding how a man of such genealogy and means could find success with such a specimen of the opposite sex.”

With a perplexed look, Miss Bev asked, “What did she just say?”

Miss Carla Mae answered, “Basically she’s wondering how in the cornbread dickens he landed such a hot to trot woman.”

The small huddle of ladies almost spit their tea out at her comment.

* * *

Benjamin

As the day went on, Benjamin thought the rodeo team seemed anxious to get back to business at hand, and that business was helping Sheriff Russell. They all agreed it was time to head over to the No Gotty and work on their plan.

As they said their goodbyes, Benjamin looked over at the head housekeeper, who was clearing plates and glasses. He realized he had seen her somewhere before but couldn't quite put his finger on where. Stopping Maddy in the foyer, he asked if she had ever seen the woman.

Maddy stood there for a few moments as she stared at the lady. Then it appeared to dawn on her, and she said, "Why, yes! She's usually down at the rodeo every weekend…which is odd, because she doesn't even have kids."

* * *

The rodeo team believed they had a secret weapon: their amateur radio licenses. So, the next order of business was to buy equipment. After they paid a quick visit to Eddie at the Ham Radio Outlet, and with his help, they purchased YAESU ham radios, antennas, and accessories and installed them in their trucks and cars.

Now, the rodeo team had a whole new world opened to them.

Maddy suggested they start keeping up with all the daily activities that went on in town.

"Write it all down on sticky notes and put it on the dry erase board in the main barn," she said. "Hopefully a pattern will emerge that we can report back to your dad, Houston."

Looking over at Maddy, Houston exclaimed, "Excellent idea! We can work out a schedule of who stakes out what area of town. We need to keep in mind that Dad thinks the drug smugglers are using the main highway through town. I suggest we start there."

Leaving the No Gotty, everyone had their marching orders, locations, and surveillance times, with an unspoken hope that this just might work. At the end of each assigned shift, the day's information was put on the board.

"Q5AGN, Q5ZPK. Q5ZPK, this is Q5AGN returning. Do we have a pathway?"

"Yes, we do, go ahead…Over."

"All is clear. Nothing out of the ordinary, unless you count the bull wagon pulling into the rodeo grounds…Over."

"Okay, thanks for the update. Be sure and put that information on the board."

"Roger, roger, will do."

"This is Q5ZKP, and I am clear."

"Q5VLN, Q5JEQ. Q5JEQ, this is Q5VLN. Go ahead."

"I am sitting over in front of the pharmacy, and I can hear the new Mrs. Weldon talking sweet to someone."

"Well, stop and think about it. She and Deputy Weldon haven't been married that long. Guess the honeymoon phase isn't over…Over."

"Q5JEQ, this is Q5BAD, and I have an update for you…Over."

"Go ahead, Q5BAD."

"Well, I am sitting around the corner from you parked in front of the real estate office, and I hate to tell you this, but Deputy Weldon isn't on his phone. As a matter of fact, he is writing a ticket to someone who evidently can't read the speed limit sign…Over."

"Who got caught speeding? Over."

"It's me! That's how I know…and my mom is gonna kill me! Over."

"Then who is Mrs. Weldon talking to?"

"Good question. Over."

"Whoever gets back to the No Gotty first, write it down on the board. Over."

"Will do, this is Q5VLN. Clear."

"Q5JEQ, clear."

"Q5BAD, clear."

After meeting up at the No Gotty to compare notes, the team was more confused than when they first began.

Mail truck came through.

Mrs. Weldon is talking sweet to someone, and it isn't her new husband.

Prayer Chain ladies going to church.

There goes Willy on his bicycle.

Prayer Chain ladies going home from church.

Bull wagon goes through town every Thursday heading to rodeo grounds.

Willy riding his bicycle to the rodeo grounds and all over town.

Deputy's making his rounds.

Florist making deliveries.

Mrs. Weldon buying gas, a lot of gas.

Food truck deliveries to the cafés.

Everyone looked at each other, bewildered.

Houston said, "What are we missing? This looks like a bunch of scrambled-up nonsense!"

Jumping up, Bubba hollered, "Saddle bags!"

Everyone stared at Bubba with confused expressions. Ariel asked, "Saddle bags? Have you lost your mind? What are you talking about?"

"Okay, look at our board," Bubba continued. "What name do you see the most of?"

Looking back over everything, Houston spoke up, "Looks like it's Willy riding that bicycle all over town."

"Exactly," Bubba replied, "and what does he have on his bicycle?"

It appeared that the lightbulbs went off in everyone's heads at the same time.

"Saddle bags!" they all shouted.

Standing up to take a bow, Bubba smiled and said, "No applause, just throw money!"

The whole rodeo team, including Benjamin, began hollering, "Yeah! We did it! Teamwork makes the dream work!"

"Wait, wait, wait, hold up," Bubba said, interrupting the celebration. "What do we do now?"

Houston responded, "Now, we take our evidence to my dad."

Benjamin couldn't wait.

Chapter 15

Houston

Houston was almost out of breath as he entered his dad's office. The Sheriff jumped up after seeing his son's disheveled appearance and asked if anything was wrong.

"No, sir. As a matter of fact, it's great news, Dad," Houston said.

He went on to tell his dad about the rodeo team's plan, as well as the fact that they had found hard evidence as to who the criminal was that the Sheriff had been searching for.

With a shocked look on his face, Houston's dad sat back down in his chair and encouraged his son to catch his breath and lay out this so-called evidence.

Houston was so proud of all the work the rodeo team had done, and he proceeded to tell the Sheriff how they came up with their info using ham radios.

"You used your ham radios?" his dad asked.

"Yes, sir, we did what you call old-fashioned police work," Houston said.

"Okay, okay," the Sheriff said. "I'm impressed, son. Let's hear what you have."

"Number one," Houston began, "Willy is not sleeping on a park bench or under the overpass. Our research shows that he rented a room. Number two, he is riding around town on a bicycle and not walking like he used to do. Number three, his bicycle has saddle bags on it. You don't see that much anymore. What's in those saddle bags?"

"Good question," his dad interjected.

"Number four," Houston continued, "he's always at the rodeos. And finally, number five—he is always riding up and down the highway that goes through town. Is that enough, Dad?"

The Sheriff thought for a second, then said, "Come to think of it, I have seen Willy on numerous occasions in the cafés around town actually buying his meal and not waiting for the day's leftovers to be offered to him. I agree there's enough evidence to bring him in for questioning. With the County Judge breathing down my neck, at least bringing in a suspect will look like we're making some progress on the case. Good work, son."

* * *

Deputy Barry

It didn't take long for the deputies to find Willy, as everyone knew all his hangout spots. When the arresting deputy, a young man named Barry, confronted him and grabbed his arm suddenly, Willy's eyes stared off, as if his mind went somewhere else, and the only thing he would say was a name they had never heard before and a bunch of numbers. No one could make heads nor tails of what the numbers meant.

After putting him in the back of the squad car and looking at him in the rearview mirror, the blank expression on Willy's face startled Deputy Barry. He tried to reassure Willy that Sheriff Russell only needed to ask him some questions, but it was like the lights were on but no one was home.

Once Deputy Barry transported Willy to the Sheriff's Office, he was surprised to learn that he already had visitors. He was especially surprised to see that those visitors were two ladies from the Prayer Chain, Miss Betty Sue and Miss Clara Mae.

Deputy Barry was quick to say hello. "Good afternoon, ladies," he said. "What brings you to the Sheriff's Office on this lovely day?"

As Miss Betty Sue and Miss Clara Mae approached the desk, he could see the look of discontent on both of their faces. Growing up in this small town, he knew exactly what that meant. Swallowing hard, and with a slight shake to his voice, he asked, "How may I help you ladies?"

Miss Betty Sue spoke up, addressing the Deputy by his first name. "Barry, where is Willy?" she asked.

This question caught Deputy Barry off guard, and a confused look spread across his face. He replied, "Ma'am, it's Deputy Barry, and why are you asking about him?"

Before Miss Betty Sue could respond, Miss Clara Mae stepped up and said, "Because he's our gigolo, and we want him back."

Deputy Barry couldn't hide the shock from his face. He began stuttering, "He's your w-what?"

"Barry, do you have peanut butter in your ears, sweetie? I said, he's our gigolo. He takes care of us, and we pay him."

Miss Betty Sue reached up, petting Miss Clara Mae on top of her gloved hand, and said, "Sister, please, let me handle this."

Smiling while adjusting her hat, Miss Clara Mae stepped back.

"Barry, what she is trying to say," Miss Betty Sue continued, "is he does all our projects and repairs around the farm, and we pay him. He has been doing these odd jobs for the past few months."

"Oh, okay, I see," the Deputy replied, feeling relieved.

Miss Clara Mae responded irritably, "Like I already told you, Barry, he takes care of us, and we pay him."

Miss Betty Sue just stood there, rolling her eyes at Miss Clara Mae's contribution to the conversation.

Deputy Barry asked the ladies to wait for a few minutes while he consulted with the Sheriff. As he walked away, he muttered under his breath, "It's Deputy Barry."

Just as Deputy Barry entered the Sheriff's office, he could hear Deputy Weldon saying Willy's fingerprints had just come back. Weldon was saying, "You're not going to believe this. He's a veteran, and a decorated one at that. Those numbers he kept saying were his social security number that the military uses for identification. Also, Willy is not his name."

Sheriff Russell seemed to notice that Deputy Barry had entered the room. He spoke up, asking, "What do you need, Deputy?"

"Sir, it sounds like I have more bad news for you," Deputy Barry said reluctantly as he relayed the conversation he'd just had with the Prayer Chain ladies. He ended the debrief with, "Looks like all the money Willy has is from working for Miss Betty Sue and Miss Clara Mae."

The feeling of defeat began to take over the room. Deputy Weldon said, "Sheriff, would you like for me to call the County Judge and give him an update?"

Hanging his head down for a moment while sighing with what sounded like disgust, Sheriff Russell replied, "No, sir, that's my job…a job I am not looking forward to, I can assure you."

Deputy Barry spoke up again, "Sheriff Russell, what do you want us to do with Willy? Let him go?"

"That's a good question, Deputy," he replied. "Seems to me that this veteran has, for whatever reason, fallen through the cracks and needs medical assistance. I've seen his look before. It's called the thousand-yard stare. Oftentimes, veterans who have been in combat are dealing with PTSD. I believe it's our responsibility to get him help. We need to reach out to the Veterans Administration Hospital and find out how they can help him."

"Yes, sir," Deputy Barry responded. "I am on it." Stopping right at the office door, Deputy Barry turned around and added, "One more thing, Sheriff. What do you want me to tell the two Prayer Chain ladies out front?"

Sheriff Russell said, "Tell them not to worry. We are going to get some help for Willy, and I am sure he will be back soon."

"Yes, sir. Sir…why have we called him Willy all this time?"

The Sheriff responded, "Growing up, I remember asking that same question to my dad, and he told me no one really knew his name. But it had become a common question around town…'Will he' be sleeping under the bridge, 'will he' be hanging out at the cafés waiting for a handout. And from that, he became known as 'Willy.' Everyone started calling him that, and Willy never argued and just began answering to that name. All these years, and we're just now finding out who he really is—a decorated combat veteran living right under our noses."

* * *

Sheriff Russell

As he finally pulled into his driveway later that night, Sheriff Russell was glad the day was over.

Just like on many other late nights throughout the years, his wife and son were waiting up for him. Sheriff Russell walked in the back door, set down his briefcase, and put his hat on the hat rack. He was relieved to be home.

As if waiting in anticipation, Houston said, "Well, Dad, how did it go with Willy? Did he confess?"

The Sheriff felt so proud of his son for trying to help, and he hated having to burst Houston's sleuthing bubble. He said, "Son, Willy has an unbreakable alibi. He is definitely not our drug transporting criminal. While I do appreciate you and your rodeo team's help…Well, son, I am asking y'all to step back and let the department handle this from now on, okay?"

"Dad, we had all the clues that pointed to Willy! This doesn't make any sense to me."

"Houston," his dad replied, "many times, clues can be misread or misunderstood, and sometimes we miss the smallest details. For you and the rodeo team's safety, please let the professionals handle this problem."

Houston answered sadly, "Yes, sir, I understand."

* * *

Houston

After school the next day, Houston got on his ham radio and called the team to an emergency meeting down at the No Gotty. He brought the team up to speed on their miscalculations about Willy being a criminal, and how the case blew up in his dad's face.

Breaking the deafening sound of silence, Ariel asked, "So, now what do we do?"

After considerable conversations, the rodeo team decided it was back to the drawing board. They assigned each team member another schedule of watching people, places, and things.

"Houston," Benjamin said, "do you remember when you told me about the sayings that American Hat Company posts online, including '+x'?"

"Sure, I do," was Houston's response.

Continuing, Benjamin said, "Well, did you read it today?" Houston shook his head no, so Benjamin went on, "It said, and I quote, 'Every day is a chance to begin again. Don't focus on the failures of yesterday; start today with positive thoughts and expectations.'"

There was a silence amongst the group. Then, Houston said, "I say we keep going… Do we all agree?"

In unison, everyone hollered out, "We agree!"

Several weeks went by, and the rodeo team continued to survey the town of any activity. After a while, they met back up at the feed barn to compare all their notes.

Feeling helpless, Houston asked, "Does anybody have anything, anything at all they can contribute? Like my dad said, it could be the smallest clue, possibly something we overlooked."

Houston couldn't help but notice Benjamin looked like he was debating something in his head. Again, Houston pleaded with the team for any information, no matter how small it seemed. According to his dad, even the smallest little detail could make a world of difference.

When it was clear no one was going to speak up, Houston said, "Okay, let's all go home and get some rest. Remember, tomorrow night we put our experiment into action."

Chapter 16

Benjamin

Friday came, and as the rodeo team started arriving at the rodeo grounds, they saw that the bull wagon in question was backed up close to the pole with steps, used by maintenance workers to replace the flood lights at the top. Benjamin and Greg agreed it would be best if they waited until later that evening, when the sun went down.

Walking around the grounds, Benjamin thought it felt like just another rodeo. The stands were full of people cheering on fellow contestants. There were parents and family members screaming at the top of their lungs when their child competed. As Greg and Benjamin walked past the concession stand, they saw Mrs. Weldon's housekeeper, Mrs. Moore, again.

Benjamin remarked to Greg, "Don't you think that's odd?"

Greg replied, "Benjamin, my friend, number one–there's a lot of people here who don't have kids. They just want to see a rodeo. And two–why does it matter? Keep your mind on the whole reason we're here."

"You're right, sorry," was Benjamin's response.

Under the cover of night, when they knew the night light would be coming on, the boys made their way through the holding pens in the back, at the far side of the trailer. It was relatively easy to climb up the fence and shimmy up the pole reaching the top of the bull wagon. Sitting his backpack down gently on the trailer, Greg set about taking everything out and getting it installed.

"What is all this?" Benjamin asked.

"It's a transceiver, small solar panel, battery, and a magnetic antenna," Greg answered back. "Everything we need for our little experiment."

Benjmain looked down at all the items Greg had taken out of his backpack. "I don't have a clue, but if you say so, that's good enough for me!"

Benjamin stopped what he was doing and started paying attention to the announcer. The announcer was saying, "Ladies and gentlemen, I have been asked to give a special message from Maddy to her new boyfriend. And while I don't understand it, we are always happy to help new love, so here goes: Horsey, Unicorn, Romeo, Romeo, Yankee." Laughing a little bit over the sound system, the announcer added, "Like I said, guess I will never understand young love."

Looking over at Greg, Benjamin asked, "What is Maddy up to? Horsey, Unicorn, Romeo, Romeo, Yankee? That doesn't make any sense. She's supposed to be standing guard."

After a few seconds, Greg said, "It makes perfectly good sense. Don't you get it? She's trying to use the phonetic alphabet to get us a message: HURRY!"

"Okay, that makes sense now, but what about the 'new boyfriend' part? Who's the new boyfriend, you or me?" Benjamin asked.

In a frantic voice, Greg whispered, "Right now, I don't know, and I don't care. We have to get this transceiver in place and get off this bull wagon before we get caught."

"How are we gonna get this transceiver to stay on top of the trailer?" Benjamin said.

"I went to an expert for help," Greg said. "I contacted Mr. Rex, W5EAK, on the radio. Come to find out, he had just the answer we needed. Evidently, back in Vietnam, they needed to attach some things to airplanes, Hueys (helicopters), his PBR (Patrol Boat, River), and they needed a way to secure it. He told me to go get a certain tape; they called it 200-mile-an-hour tape. If it worked for him, surely it will work for us."

"Man, what did you tell him you needed it for?" Benjamin asked.

"That was easy," Greg said. "I told him we were conducting a test, showing the team how we can follow not only vehicles, but a trailer, too."

With the last piece of tape in place, Greg looked over at Benjamin and said, "All done. Now all we do is wait for this trailer to move, and we can track it."

Smiling a big grin, Benjamin said, "Let's get off this bull wagon before we're caught."

The two boys barely got off the trailer, slipping over behind the holding pens, when they heard voices approaching. Grabbing Benjamin by the arm, Greg said, "Let's get out of here."

But Benjamin froze and said, "Wait a minute. That voice is familiar. I've got to see their face to be sure."

Greg agreed, "Okay, but take your hat off so they don't see the brim of it and give our position away."

"Good idea," Benjamin said, and he did so.

Peeking around the gate, Benjamin looked at the two men who had walked over to the bull wagon. He couldn't be sure just yet, as the men were standing mostly in the shadows.

"Man, you look like you just saw a ghost," Greg remarked. "Are you okay?"

"Greg, I may have seen a ghost, and I think that ghost is worthy of a sticky note on our board."

With that, Benjamin and Greg crept away and made it back to their teammates. As they walked past them, they gave the signal that everything was in place; mission accomplished!

However, when they found Maddy, the boys had some questions for her about her strange announcement. "Sorry, guys," she said, "but a couple of the stock contractors were talking about whether they needed to replace a couple of clearance lights now or at the truck stop when they stopped to fuel up. Guess I panicked."

"Okay, but what was all that boyfriend stuff about?" Greg asked.

Maddy's face turned red. She quickly responded, "Don't have a clue what you're talking about. I gotta go get ready for my event."

Benjamin and Greg started shoving each other.

"It's you!"

"No, it's you!"

Clearly, Maddy had two admirers who were afraid to admit it.

Chapter 17

Greg

At the next rodeo meeting, the kids could barely wait until Greg gave them an update on their little test that they put into motion at last week's rodeo. After roll call, everyone knew it was time for him to give his report.

"My data," Greg began, "shows the bull wagon coming from our southern border, where we all know a lot of the bulls, steer wrestling, and roping cattle come from. Here are all the points he stopped at."

The rodeo team was clearly impressed with this part of the ham radio systems at their fingertips. They could see it all in real time on Greg's computer.

Taping the printed map up on their board, Greg continued, "Just like I promised, a printout of his route. As you can see, the bull wagon makes a run from our southern border to pick up the fresh livestock, and then it makes its rounds through what we know as the rodeo circuit for our region. Looks to me like it's the same exact route every week."

Scratching his head before putting his hat back on, Bubba asked, "Wouldn't it help if we had more information about the places that he stops at?"

"Good point," Maddy said.

"It's simple," Greg responded. "All we have to do is look where he is stopping on the map."

After a little research, every stop the bull wagon made became clear. "After each rodeo, it appears that the bull wagon stopped at the nearest roadside park," Greg said.

He murmured to himself, "Stop." It seemed that the only thing his other rodeo teammates heard was "rodeo," and they were all talking about their hopes of competing at that arena one day.

"Hold up a minute!" Greg shouted. "We're so excited about the rodeo circuit that we completely missed the part where he is pulling into these roadside parks for only 10 minutes each time! This doesn't make a lick of sense at all!"

Catching everyone off guard with this new information, the room fell silent.

Ariel spoke up, "I can see stopping at a truck stop, but not a roadside park that often. Something sounds fishy to this cowgirl."

Everyone nodded their heads in agreement. Bubba said, "I think we need to follow him, at least just to our roadside park after the rodeo next weekend."

The whole room erupted into opinions.

Stepping up onto a bale of hay, Houston whistled the loudest he had ever whistled in his life to get his rodeo family's attention. Houston hollered, "Okay, guys! Bubba is right; if we are gonna find out anything past what Greg's printout tells us, we will have to follow him. Before you vote yes or no, know this: it could go past our curfews, we may be driving farther out of town than we are supposed to, and if we get caught, well... We all may be grounded until we graduate college."

Raising his hand, Benjamin asked if he could speak. "Come on up here," Houston said as he reached out a hand to help Benjamin up.

"The way I see it is this," Benjamin started. "We are a rodeo family... one for all and all for one! I say we are in this together! And besides that, if we do get caught, well... College isn't that far away."

The whole room burst out laughing. "Next weekend it is!" they agreed.

* * *

Just like clockwork, as the rodeo winded down, the bull wagon and other trailers full of rough stock would begin leaving the rodeo grounds to head out. However, this time, they would have company. Traveling a safe distance away so as not to be spotted, it wasn't hard for the rodeo team to keep the large trailer with all those clearance lights in their sight.

Taking no chances, the rodeo team changed their positions by talking on their radios so that one of them was in front, one was on the side, and one was following the rear of the trailer. They had no intentions of letting this bull wagon get away.

"Q5JEQ, Q5AGN…"

"Q5JEQ here. Go ahead, Q5AGN."

"Taking the lead position; you move back to the side."

"Roger, roger…Greg…moving back to the side."

Looking down at his notes, Greg realized that the first normal stop should be at the upcoming roadside park—that is, if his route stayed true to the last APRS report.

"Q5AGN…Q5ZKP, looks like he's moving over to take the exit."

"Q5ZKP…Q5AGN will drop back to the rear."

"Q5VLNL…Q5AGN."

"Q5VLN…Go ahead, Q5AGN. Exit ahead of him and pull to the back behind the vending machines."

"Q5VLN, roger."

The rodeo team decided they should all pull in behind the vending machines, which had so much tree and shrub coverage that they were completely hidden in the shadows. With their engines off, they all sat in silence, waiting.

Greg motioned for everyone to get out and sneak over to the side of the vending machine area. As everyone gathered around, Greg told them to split up and stay in the shadows. "I think it's best if we blanket this area," he said.

"Then what?" Bubba asked.

"Well," Greg said, "I guess we just sit and wait."

The bull wagon had pulled in over to the side where trucks were supposed to park, turned off all its lights, and was sitting there in the dark. Several cars and trucks pulled into the roadside park, with some stopping to use the restroom facilities, some walking their dogs, and some just stopping to stretch their legs. After a few minutes, they all went back to their vehicles and on the road.

The rodeo team all watched a different area of the park. Ariel whispered that she had noticed a dark SUV pull into the far side of the parking lot. They had turned their lights off, unlike all the other cars, and no one got out, which seemed strange.

A few minutes later, the truck driver climbed down out of his truck, which was easy to see in the soft light surrounding the parking lot. It appeared to Greg that he was checking out the area before walking away from his rig. After a few moments, the man quickly made his way over to the dark SUV.

As he approached the driver's side of the SUV, it looked like he was carrying a brown paper bag. The driver's window went down, and he passed the paper bag through the window, handing it to someone. Then, what appeared to be a woman's hand passed another bag to him. And to top it all off, the man leaned into the window, and he and the woman's silhouette were kissing.

Greg watched as Ariel made her way in the shadows back to the rest of the team, no doubt to tell everyone what she had just seen.

"Looks like he's meeting some woman here at the roadside park is all," Ariel sighed. "All this experiment amounts to is the truck driver seeing someone. Are y'all ready to go home?"

Benjamin said, "Guys, it's worse than what we thought!"

Houston turned to Benjamin and asked, "What are you talking about?"

"That dark SUV he walked up to... Well, I recognize the funny license plate. It's a match to the one I saw at the housewarming party at Deputy Weldon's house. It was parked in their garage by the side door."

With a look of shock and grief, all the kids sat down on the curb, completely at a loss for words and not knowing what to do next.

Ariel looked over at the rest of the team and said, "Guys, I sure do feel sorry for Deputy Weldon. His heart will be broken."

The rodeo team decided they had better get home before they got caught. They all left in silence; no one said a word. Greg was so disappointed.

The next day, they were sure to put all their findings up on the board down at the No Gotty. The new notes from this surprising turn of events, however, no one was looking forward to putting on the board.

* * *

Houston

Promptly after school, Houston drove by his dad's office to see him. Walking up to Deputy Barry, he asked, "Sir, is my dad in?"

"Sure, he is," was the Deputy's response. "Go on in."

Sheriff Russell always seemed glad to see his son. Houston thought he secretly hoped that one day, he would follow in his footsteps.

The Sheriff looked at him and asked carefully, "Do you have something on your mind?" No doubt, he could tell Houston's demeanor was off.

"Yes, sir, I do," Houston replied. "Sir…can we talk?"

His dad nodded.

"Now, don't get mad, Dad," Houston began, "but me and the rodeo team were conducting an experiment using Greg's APRS, trying to figure out just how far we could track someone or something. And we have gathered a lot of information. To be honest, we now know some information we wish we didn't know."

"And what would that be, son?" Sheriff Russell asked.

"Well, sir," Houston said, "we know for sure the new Mrs. Weldon is cheating on Deputy Weldon, and to make matters worse, we know who with."

"Son, I thought I told y'all to drop your investigating," the Sheriff said sternly.

"I know, Dad, you did…And we did. It's just that we wanted to help, too. Sorry, Dad, I know you are disappointed in me and the team."

The Sheriff sat in silence for a moment before saying, "Okay, son. It's too late to cry over spilled milk, so fill me in on this new information y'all found."

"Dad," Houston continued, "we went back to our notes, and we have a lot of them. What we discovered was that the new Mrs. Weldon, about every other night or so, was filling up that big black SUV at the gas station. I thought those things got better gas mileage than that."

Nodding his head in agreement, the Sheriff said, "That's true, son. I'm proud that you took initiative here, though I'm a little upset you didn't listen to me. To be honest, I'm not sure whether to ground you or hug you."

Houston smiled at that.

After another moment, Sheriff Russell said, "How about we go down to the No Gotty and take a look at your notes?"

"Yes, sir," Houston replied.

* * *

Sheriff Russell

Walking into the feed room, Sheriff Russell could see all the intense and lengthy work his son and the rodeo team had put into helping him crack this case. As a matter of fact, it touched the Sheriff's heart.

Looking over at his son, he said, "Okay, lay it out for me, son. Show me what y'all got."

Houston was quick to lay out their plan—how they had sat down and figured out a schedule where everybody took turns on a rotation, watching anybody and anything that came through the main highway running through the center of their town. They had felt sure they could come up with some clues.

"Some of the sticky notes," Houston explained, "were from when we thought Willy was the drug smuggler, and then some of our notes prove that the new Mrs. Weldon, well…Let's just say she was sweet talking someone on the phone, and it wasn't Deputy Weldon. We have it all documented—the times that she was constantly getting gas, especially on the nights that we knew Deputy Weldon was on duty. Sir, it didn't make sense to us, but facts are facts, and like you always say, Dad, sometimes it's the small details that can crack a case wide open."

Looking closer at the sticky notes taped to the dry erase board, something caught the Sheriff's eye. "Are you sure about these dates and times, son?" he asked.

Houston responded, "Oh yes, sir, we are very sure about every bit of it. We called it into our, well, what Miss Donna, W5SML, calls her 'Secret Command Center.' She helped us gather all the information. Why do you ask, Dad?"

"Well, to be honest with you, I know for a fact that the new Mrs. Weldon couldn't have been at some of those dates and times, as she was attending community functions and parties. She was highly visible there all through the evening."

"How do you know that for sure?" Houston asked.

Glancing back over his shoulder from the board at his son, Sheriff Russell answered, "Because I was part of the security detail that night and saw her with my own eyes."

Taking his hat off and scratching his head, Houston responded, "That doesn't make any sense, Dad. How can she be in two places at the same time?"

"I agree with you, son, which tells me there is a little bit more to this story than what meets the eye. As a matter of fact, I believe this rodeo team has just cracked the case."

"Are you kidding me, Dad? Do you really mean it?" Houston asked.

"Yes, I do," Sheriff Russell replied. "But before I can say anything, there's something I need to check out."

About this time, the rest of the rodeo team started showing up to get ready for practice. As they walked into the feed room, Houston told them the great news: "My dad said we have helped him crack this case wide open!"

With looks of excitement on their faces, all eyes turned to the Sheriff.

Sheriff Russell thanked the rodeo team for all their hard work and dedication in helping their community, and he went on to say that, now, it was time to lay the real trap.

Greg spoke up, "Sir, we still have the transceiver on top of the trailer."

With a grin, the Sheriff responded back, "Well, son, that's good to know. First," he continued, pointing up at the printout that was taped to the barn wall, "how did y'all get the map the bull wagon followed?" Everyone looked over at Greg, so the Sheriff asked, "Greg, son, do you know?"

"Yes, sir," Greg said. "As a matter of fact, I did it with my APRS system when we were doing an experiment to see where a car, truck, or trailer would travel."

Holding his hand up as if to tell Greg to stop for a second, the Sheriff asked, "Son, what is an APRS system? What does it do?"

Greg replied, "The short story, sir, is this: it's a transceiver connected to a GPS sending out its position on a regular timed interval. I can follow it in real time on my computer, which shows me elevation, speed, and direction. With this information, we know everything that the transceiver is attached to. It was just a fun experiment, sir, that's all. I promise."

"Okay, son, you're not in trouble," Sheriff Russell assured him. "I just need to ask another question. Does the route ever change?"

Greg said, "No, sir, it's been the same route for several weeks now, or at least since the rodeo season started."

Addressing the whole rodeo team, Sheriff Russell said, "This is some very good police work y'all have done. How about helping me out with another experiment?"

With a surprised look on his face, Houston shouted out, "Heck yes! Just tell us what to do, Dad."

"I will let y'all know when I am ready to have a meeting about our experiment. And on that note, I am heading back to the office so y'all can get to your practice tonight."

* * *

The following week seemed to drag by, as everyone anticipated the coming weekend.

Finally, the Sheriff sent word to meet down at his office. When the rodeo team arrived, they were ushered into a big conference room that they had seen many times on TV from the evening news whenever the Sheriff was being interviewed.

Taking a seat, everyone looked anxious to hear the big plan. Luckily, they didn't have to wait very long, as the Sheriff and several deputies came in through the side door.

Laying out the plan for Friday night after the rodeo, it was pretty much the same plan the rodeo team had, but with a few special caveats. The Sheriff's plan began with deputies already being in place, along with a lady deputy who would act as a decoy. After his presentation, the Sheriff asked if there were any questions…and there weren't.

The Sheriff concluded, "Okay then, we are good to go for Friday night."

Most of the time, a rodeo seemed to pass by too quicky. However, this night, it dragged on and on for everyone involved. Finally, the time came for the bull wagons to start pulling out.

As Greg looked over at Houston, he said, "And the game's afoot!"

With a confused look on his face, Houston asked, "What did you just say?"

Laughing out loud, Greg said, "Never mind. I will explain it later."

With everyone in place, it was just a matter of time before the bull wagon arrived at the roadside park, according to previous APRS data.

There were deputies dressed as maintenance workers sweeping the area around the bathrooms and vending machines. One was picking up trash, and a couple of others were walking their dogs and stretching their legs like travelers.

As the rodeo team pulled in and went to the back to park and hide in the shadows, Benjamin pointed out, "Look, there's the black SUV in the same parking space as last time."

With everyone in place, it was now a waiting game.

The sound of air brakes quickly got the attention of all involved in this sting operation. And just like before, the bull wagon driver pulled into almost the exact same parking space as he had the week before. Within minutes, the driver stepped out of his truck, while obviously watching his surroundings. He was holding what looked like another brown paper bag. Just like before, he began making his way towards the dark SUV that sat in the shadows. As the driver's window rolled down, you could hear him saying, "Here's the money. Give me more candy."

As they exchanged packages, the driver began to lean in through the window to get his kiss, as he did before. Then, out of nowhere, everyone heard, "Pucker up, sweetie, and come to momma!"

To his shock, two much older, arthritic hands grabbed his face and kissed him like he was leaving for war!

Shocked by the voice that he had just heard, not to mention the kiss, the man tried to pull away and step back, but he stumbled over the curb and fell backward into the shrubs and flower bed, right into the most beautiful blooming cactus you had ever seen.

From out of the shadows, squad cars, sirens, and deputies surrounded the driver with flashing lights that were almost blinding. Looking at the prisoner who was screaming at the top of his lungs, Sheriff Russell laughed, because he figured out that the man was screaming about the cactus, which probably didn't feel too good.

With the bull wagon driver in custody, handcuffed, and sitting in the back of the squad car along with his co-driver, everybody could breathe a sigh of relief.

It was at this point the Sheriff realized the undercover female deputy had never gotten out of the black SUV. Just as he looked over to where the dark SUV was parked, he heard the engine starting up and the car backing out of its parking space. As the car came down the parking lot past him, everyone wanted to tell her good job. As the car approached, and to everyone's surprise as the dark-tinted windows rolled down, there was Miss Betty Sue and Miss Clara Mae, smiling and waving as they drove by.

Miss Clara Mae hollered out, "Talk to you later, guys! We must get home; it's almost time for our favorite show to come on!" Without waiting for the Sheriff's reply, they tore out of the parking lot and headed home.

Sheriff Russell started laughing all over again. Deputy Weldon asked him, "What's so funny?"

Catching his breath, the Sheriff said, "I really don't know if the man was screaming from the cactus on his backside or the kiss he got from Miss Betty Sue."

After composing himself, the Sheriff remarked, "Looks like we got half the smuggling team. Now, let's go get the rest of them."

Chapter 18

Houston

As he headed out the door, Houston's mom hollered, "Your dad forgot his lunch again! Can you please drop it off for me?"

"Sure thing, Mom," Houston replied. "I am going right by his office on the way to the No Gotty."

After Houston walked into the front office of the Police Department, Deputy Barry looked up from his paperwork and laughed, saying, "Again?"

"Yes, sir, again," Houston said. He was about to leave, having done what he came there to do, but then he overheard his dad's voice on the radio at the dispatch desk.

The Sheriff was saying, "Car 14 to base. I have arrested our suspect. I am bringing her in."

Houston gasped and ran out the door to get on his ham radio so that he could tell everyone what he just heard. Within minutes, the whole rodeo team showed up, waiting for the Sheriff to arrive and to watch the new Mrs. Weldon be escorted in handcuffs from the squad car to a jail cell.

Standing there with anticipation and feeling proud of themselves, they were all in shock when it wasn't Mrs. Weldon after all. It Mrs. Moore, the housekeeper, doing the walk of shame!

As Houston and the team looked at the Sheriff with a perplexed expression, Sheriff Russell said, "I will explain later. Let me turn the prisoner over to Deputy Barry for booking."

Everyone anxiously awaited an explanation of what was going on. Finally, Sheriff Russell came back out to talk to them. "Remember when you asked me to come down to the No Gotty to look at y'all's notes?" he asked Houston.

"Yes, sir, I do," Houston replied.

"Well, when I saw the rodeo team's notes on the board, everything started moving around in my mind. This whole puzzle started falling into place. Your notes were the key to this whole case: from Willy to Benjamin's dog barking at only one of the bull wagons, to Mrs. Weldon's black SUV using so much gas, to Benjamin thinking he saw someone from his past, to people getting speeding tickets, to people talking sweet to those they weren't married to."

The rodeo team stood there in silence, hanging onto every word the Sheriff told them.

He went on, "My first order of business was to call the Stock Contractor about his truck drivers and other hired help. Come to find out, he had only hired the one driver just before the rodeo season kicked off, and guess what his name is? Gus Addison. So, Benjamin, you did see who you thought you saw. After doing a background check on him, I discovered Mr. Addison isn't the type to win an outstanding citizen award. Far from it. He has a rap sheet as long as your arm and my arm put together.

"From the many functions I have attended at Deputy Weldon's home, I also realized that the new Mrs. Weldon and Mrs. Moore looked a whole like alike: similar height, weight, and hair color, especially from the back, and that is what y'all saw on different nights at the gas station in town. After checking credit card statements, while the new Mrs. Weldon does use a lot of gas, she wasn't the only one driving the black SUV. Some nights, it was the new Mrs. Weldon, and some nights, it was Mrs. Moore. It turns out, Mrs. Moore was meeting up with some of her local dealers. With the two women looking so much alike, especially from a distance, the soft glow of the parking lot lights played tricks on your eyes.

"I realized Mrs. Weldon couldn't have been in all the places you kids saw her, sometimes getting gas and sometimes walking around to the back of the convenience store. Working on a hunch, at the next function I attended, I took a glass Mrs. Moore had handled. Bringing it back to the police station, there were fingerprints to run, and I soon discovered her name is not Mrs. Moore. It is, in fact, Helen Addison, the wife of Gus Addison. She and her husband were under suspicion and were persons of interest, but no one could prove how they transported the drugs. As it turns out, that was all due to a man Benjamin knew as 'Uncle Gus.' Then, I did a little checking on your dog, Benjamin."

"On Foster?" Benjamin asked.

"Yes, sir," the Sheriff said. "I did a little digging, and guess what, son? You are the proud owner of a retired drug sniffing dog."

Looking over at the team, Benjamin exclaimed, "Wow! I knew something was up with Foster!"

Sheriff Russell went on, "Kids, as you can see, Deputy Weldon is not here right now. He is overseeing the transporting of our two main criminals to the DEA office. Which gives me an opportunity to talk with you. It would appear that while the new Mrs. Weldon does use a lot of gas, we know she is not meeting up with the drug smugglers, which means we have no proof that she is cheating on Deputy Weldon. We only have proof that she does a lot of driving at night, especially when Deputy Weldon is on duty. So, I strongly suggest we keep all that information to ourselves as it is only circumstantial at best. Agreed?"

Before anyone could say anything, Ariel exclaimed, "Sir, something is going on, and we are worried about Deputy Weldon."

Seeing the look of compassion in her face, the Sheriff responded, "What the new Mrs. Weldon is doing is between her and Deputy Weldon. End of story. It's none of our business, agreed?"

The entire team looked at each other and finally looked over at the Sheriff. With their fingers crossed behind their backs, all of them said in unison, "Yes, sir, agreed."

"Good deal," Sheriff Russell said. "I think this is the right decision for now. Now, I think it's time for all of us to go get ready for the town celebration tonight. I hear the Prayer Chain is making all the refreshments!"

* * *

Sheriff Russell

Later that evening found almost everyone at the town's community center, celebrating not only the arrest of the drug smuggling ring, but also a surprise birthday party for Benjamin. Everyone anxiously waited for Sheriff Russell to reveal what had happened.

Standing there in amazement at how this all played out, the Prayer Chain, like everyone else in the room, hung onto every word the Sheriff spoke. He laid out how the drug smugglers were caught due to all the good police work the rodeo team had undertaken, their facts, and their notes. The whole time, the rodeo team stood there so proud to have been a part of helping protect their community and get those drugs off the streets.

The Prayer Chain was preparing the birthday cake and punch when Miss Shelly Belle spoke up and said, "Due to his analytical shortcomings, it would appear that this ruffian 'Uncle Gus' was overwhelmed through cranial flatulating, followed by probable air leaks of the temporal lobe."

Looking over at Miss Clara Mae, the Sheriff asked, "What did she say?"

Miss Clara Mae responded, "She said that lawless idiot evidently had multiple brain farts!"

With a nod of Anne Richards' head to Miss Betty Sue, giving the Prayer Chain the cue to roll out the birthday cake with all the trimmings, the Richards spoke up and said, "We are also here to celebrate Benjamin's birthday today."

With a surprised look on his face, Benjamin shouted, "A party for me?"

Anne walked up to Benjamin and said, "We have two gifts for you." She handed him a box that said "Gift #1" on it. Standing there holding this beautifully wrapped birthday present, Benjamin appeared frozen in time, clearly not wanting this moment to end.

"Go on," Anne urged him, "open your gift."

The Sheriff watched the boy unwrap the box carefully, and he pulled out several papers stapled together.

Not to be left out of this great celebration, the County Judge stepped up and said, "Benjamin, I am honored to say I played a part in this first gift."

Benjamin asked, "What are these papers for? I don't understand."

Anne took Benjamin's hand, looked into his eyes, and said through a tearful voice, "You are just like our son—that is, if you want to be. These are adoption papers."

Benjamin stared at the Richards, his foster parents, with tears in his eyes. He said, "All I've ever wanted was to have a family, and now I do: a rodeo family, a mom, and a dad. I'm the luckiest boy in the world."

Then, Anne handed him the second box marked "Gift #2." With a smile the size of Texas, Benjamin was again very careful with the wrapping paper. His rodeo team was hollering, "Hurry up! Open it! What is it?"

With yet another confused look, Benjamin exclaimed as he pulled the gift out, "I have no idea what this is! I think it's an old polaroid picture." He looked over at his new mom and dad. "What is this?"

Smiling through tears of joy, Anne explained, "You're going to be a big brother."

Everyone in the room broke out cheering and clapping, including Sheriff Russell, smiling and hollering congratulations, as they all knew the Richards had been dealing with being told they could not have children of their own.

Miss Betty Sue hollered out, "What a wonderful night of celebration! Answered prayers all around!"

Between the music playing in the background, people enjoying the refreshments along with cake and ice cream, and small kids running around playing, happiness was in full bloom on this wonderful evening. The community center was alive with laughter and congratulations.

As the evening's festivities were in full swing, the Sheriff walked over to the Prayer Chain ladies to ask them how they knew to be there during their little experiment, to which Miss Betty Sue responded, "QSL!"

Anne leaned over and asked Benjamin, "Son, what does that mean?"

Answering his new mother, Benjamin said, "It means I confirm or acknowledge that I heard."

"Okay, ladies," the Sheriff spoke up, "I am asking you again. How, when, where, and what did you hear?"

Miss Betty Sue answered, "We heard that your undercover officer had a little fender bender and was not going to make it to the stakeout on time. We then realized your undercover officer was driving a black SUV. We have a dark SUV, and in the shadows of the night, they can easily be mistaken for one another. Figured we could lend a helping hand, so to speak."

With a confused look on his face, the Sheriff turned to both Miss Betty Sue and Miss Clara Mae and asked, "Exactly how did you know that?"

Miss Clara Mae said, "Oh, a little birdie on the airwaves told us!"

The rodeo team, Rex, and Donna seemed to know exactly what Miss Clara Mae meant. As Rex turned to Donna, the Sheriff heard Rex whisper, "Evidently the Prayer Chain has a little secret, and I think we both know what it is."

Donna responded quietly, "Yes, sir, I agree with you. Like many people have said, there is more to the Prayer Chain ladies than what meets the eye."

As the evening's celebration continued, the Sheriff and County Judge struck up a conversation at the party.

"You know, Sheriff," the County Judge said, "your team has done an outstanding job of bringing these criminals to justice, and I commend you on a job well done."

"Your Honor," Sheriff Russell said, "to be totally transparent with you, I must admit we got most of our clues from the high school rodeo kids using their ham radios."

"Well, Sheriff," the Judge continued, "then I suggest this might be something your office looks into for themselves."

With a mouth full of delicious birthday cake, all the Sheriff could do was nod his head in agreement.

"Well, let's just say it was a big collaboration on solving this case, shall we?" the Judge winked at Sheriff Russell. "Bottom line is this: looks like our little community can go back to being a small, quiet town with less crime."

The Sheriff said, "We have solved the drug trafficking issue in our town, for now. However, there is still the new wife of Deputy Weldon, and that is another story. I highly suspect there is more to that than we know."

With a concerned look on his face, the County Judge responded back, "Sheriff, I would hate to lose a good man like Deputy Weldon, so I suggest you quietly look into this matter."

After a few moments of thinking, the Sheriff replied, "Agreed, sir, agreed."

Neither man knew that anyone had been listening in on their conversation. However, two of the Prayer Chain ladies were standing on the other side of the paper-thin room divider and overheard every word. Not wasting any time, they immediately gathered the rest of the Prayer Chain in the kitchen to relay the conversation in its entirety.

"Well, ladies," Miss Betty Sue said quietly under her breath, "looks like we know our next mission!"

With all the food put away, tables cleaned off, and chairs stacked, it was time to call it a night. Sheriff Russell waited patiently at the front door for everyone to leave so that he could lock up.

As the Prayer Chain ladies exited the party, he overheard Miss Shelly Belle say, "To the credit of amateur radio, physics, geography, mathematics, and social science, it would appear that the flow of illegal contraband has been seriously interrupted at this moment in time in our town. However, the issue of the recent nuptials of our newest citizen, as well as her financial standing, well…That remains to be seen."

Sheriff Russell looked over at Miss Clara Mae to ask, "What did she just say?"

Smiling at the Sheriff, Miss Clara Mae said, "That, my dear, is another adventure, another story."

Thank You to Readers

I sincerely hope you enjoyed the first book of the *Texas Rodeo and Radios* series, *Down at the No Gotty.* It was my intention to write a book that was wholesome, entertaining, intriguing, and an adventure you would love.

Many of the characters in this book reflect people who I have crossed paths with in my life. You may even identify with one of them as they navigate this crazy thing we call life. While growing up can be hard, it is who you travel the road with that makes all the difference in the world.

The No Gotty proves it.

Book 2 Coming Soon

Using their amateur radio and sleuthing skills, the rodeo team quickly discovers that music is indeed a national language. Can Ariel "cowgirl up" to help save the day? To reflect back on one thing Miss Donna taught, even if you have to do it scared...do it anyway!

About the Author

Donna Snow King is a proud, multi-generational Texan, born and raised in Fort Worth. Growing up a third generation house mover, which started with her Grandpa Snow in 1942, eventually led her to the TV world where she and her sister, Toni, (The Snow Sisters) were introduced to the world.

H.D. Snow and Son House Moving, Inc. has been a huge part of her life with her Daddy, H.D. Snow, her brother, and her sister. During her off time from moving houses and historical buildings, she volunteers not only at her church but also mentoring youth at the local high school rodeo associations, as well as an advocate for our Military, Veterans, and their families. Donna is happily married to the love of her life, Rex. They are enjoying life on the Snow-King Ranch. With both Donna and her husband holding Amateur Radio Licenses, you can often hear them on their Ham Radios. Their call signs are W5SML and W5EAK. Her philosophy in life is to never miss a good chance to sow a seed by helping someone.

Donna's debut book, *Snow Much Love: Book 1*, was released in 2023, and its sequel, *Snow Much Love: Book 2* was released in 2024. Both books quickly became family favorites among readers.

www.DonnaSnowKing.com

www.ingramcontent.com/pod-product-compliance
Lightning Source LLC
LaVergne TN
LVHW010952110826
845149LV00015B/3304